ROCKMOOR

First EnvisionArts paperbac

BOOK TWO OF TINDER & FLINT

WITHDRAWN

By
Matthew Hinsley

Art by
Billy Garretsen

EnvisionARTS

Austin

First EnvisionArts Paperback Edition, May 2017

Cover Design by Billy Garretsen

Author Photo by Victoria Enders

Artist Photo by John Gibson

Published by EnvisionArts, LLC.

ISBN 978-1-387-00368-6

www.tinderandflintbooks.com

For Mom & Bob

Thank you to my fellow adventurers Joe Williams II, Quentin Lucas, Joseph Palmer, Travis Marcum, Amelia Devivo, and Glenda Lee, I wouldn't want to adventure with anyone else! Thank you to my editors Jessica Hagemann, Glenda Lee, Rebecca Snedden, and Robert Knapp. Billy Garretsen: you are a great inspiration, creating this world together is a blast, and I'm looking forward to much more. And to my readers, I hope you love, love, love this deeper foray into the world of *Tinder & Flint*—it's starting to get serious!

Contents

Revealed beneath the rug, embedded in the stone itself,
was an image resembling a black bat with ruby red eyes.

Chapter One
MORDIMER

_____

Mordimer was sweating. His voice was raw from ceaseless pleading. He spent the sleepless night alternately clawing his way around the cold, dark room in search of a way out, and clutching his wife and two daughters close to him for warmth and comfort. Together their voices rose and fell through the night like a sad, poorly rehearsed chorus of feral cats.

The question they kept asking the merciless walls, and the deaf ears beyond, was why. *Why did you take us? What do you want with us? What are you going to do with us?*

No answers came.

Mordimer was positively terrified. He was terrified for them. He had had brushes with death before, and while he was not hoping to come face to face with it again any time soon, the thought of his own end was far more welcome than the injury or demise of his precious family. *Let them go!* was a regular refrain shouted throughout the damp, hellish night, often followed or preceded by, *I'll do anything you want!*

Mordimer was a big man. He was, perhaps, most at home in the woods hunting or walking in silence. As a boy he had learned to recognize the sounds and tracks of animals. He loved to follow his father on excursions into the forest. When he was orphaned at thirteen, Mordimer's size and gentle demeanor attracted the attention of other boys, particularly those bullies inclined to violence. It took only a few beatings before he learned to use his size and instincts to defend himself.

Soon after his parents' death, in desperation, he found his way to the docks of Rockmoor, whose shipyards were the heart of commerce for the bustling port city. On the afternoon of his very first day there, a jovial and corpulent captain noticed the mongrel youth skulking near a pile of fishy traps and salt-dried nets.

"Oh ho! What have we here?" the captain boomed, flapping and rolling his way to stop directly over the cowering youth. "Is there something here you'd like, boy?" His eyes glinted with worldly experience and a tinge of humor; his flowing scarlet and black silk garments billowed in the ocean breezes. "Maybe something your dirty little fingers are hoping to grab when Jastro isn't looking?" The big jovial eyes narrowed and swept the piled items on the dock in mock accusation.

Mordimer was speechless. He was frightened. He had not taken anything. If he was honest, though, he had to admit his biting hunger had prodded him to notice the valuable things on the docks that seemed easily portable.

"Come now, boy." Jastro relaxed the ruse of indignation in his voice and countenance, and allowed the faintest hint of sincerity to creep into his tone: "What is it that brings you here all by yourself?"

Perhaps it was the hunger, or perhaps the desperation—but in that moment, Mordimer found courage to answer the opulent stranger directly. This was a chance, and he hadn't had too many of those in his short, troubled life.

"A job, sir," he managed.

"A job!" cried the captain to the audience of seagulls and waves. "The boy wants a job," Jastro continued, feigning contemplation. "And where might your parents be, boy?"

"Mum and dad are dead, sir," Mordimer replied meekly.

Jastro considered this for several long moments, during which time the boy became acutely aware of the chilly wind off the sea, the noisy insistent lapping at the shore, the bobbing of the ships, and of the rigid dry mask of his own face as he squinted up hopefully at the loud seaman, the sun shining brightly above.

"I'll tell you what, boy." The man rummaged in his enormous black sequined vest. "You be here tomorrow morning at first light and we'll see if I can find something to keep you occupied." With that, he pushed two small copper coins into Mordimer's limp hands with his warm, pudgy fingers, and strode off into the city.

Mordimer woke early in the packed sand beneath the slatted wood boards of the docks. He was nervous and had slept poorly, not wanting to miss his appointment. One of the copper coins had bought him a cup of odiferous fish stew; the other coin had joined him for his fitful slumber, nestled tightly in the same hand he'd used as a pillow.

Jastro emerged at first light from a large vessel, accompanied by several strapping and exotic-looking elaborately tattooed men. He whistled to Mordimer with a beckoning flick of his wrist, and Mordimer raced to meet him. There was work to do: hard, heavy, sweaty work moving crates, carpets, fabrics, casks, and many other things. It was perfect. Almost instantly Mordimer fell into the rhythm of the simple physical labor beside the wordless sailors.

When the sun set, Mordimer was exhausted, smelly, incredibly hungry, and extremely happy. Jastro gave him four more of the copper pieces and invited him back the following morning to clear the hold of another trading vessel. That evening, the boy spent two of the coins on a larger bowl of stew and a hunk of bread. And overnight he slept soundly, holding fast to the three copper pieces he had now saved.

Through this first employment, Mordimer found other jobs loading and unloading goods of all kinds at the docks. But anytime Jastro was at port, he would drop everything to work for his mysterious benefactor. After a little over a year, he had saved enough copper to rent a tiny room at a nearby inn, where he ate, slept, and carefully saved his earnings. On slow days, he would leave the city and hunt in the dense lush forests of his youth. He often returned with the carcass of a deer or boar that he would skin, butcher, and then trade for some of the myriad treasures that flowed through the docks each day.

He met his wife one early fall afternoon when the nights were just becoming colder. He had several extra pelts stored in his room, and he knew that with the frigid air blowing in he would be able to trade them well.

She sat glumly on a blanket with a basketful of oysters in front of a dingy boat that looked barely seaworthy. A loud drunkard, her father, swayed on board and heaped derision on his other children. She stared mournfully at the ground as Mordimer approached. Mordimer was very fond of oysters, and while the whole basket wasn't worth even one of the pelts he carried, he very much fancied trying one. He was just thinking about how many coins he was carrying when she turned her gaze upward, weariness and sorrow in her huge almond-shaped eyes.

And they connected.

Taking note of the potential customer, her father became silent. When his daughter did not speak up immediately about their wares, he blundered from the boat and apologized to the stranger for his idiot-daughter's manners. He asked if the stranger might like some of the freshest oysters in all of Rockmoor. His voice grew louder and more insistent, as if hoping some other stray passerby might hear as well. He bragged about the secret place he'd gathered these oysters, a place that only he knew.

Mordimer and the girl ignored him, lost in each other's eyes.

Finally the wiry little man lumbered toward them, a storm brewing in his drunken stare. The girl tore her frightened eyes away and cowered slightly as though expecting to be struck. Mordimer intervened, "Forgive me my manners, sir. I do love oysters and I admire great beauty, and I've found both at once right here before me. I'm overcome."

Light dawned in the man's polluted mind. "She's not for sale, you sick city bastard. But for copper I'll gladly deal ya some oysters to take back wherever you come from."

For the second time in his life, Mordimer realized he was being given a chance. Chances, he had come to believe, were to be seized when offered.

Chapter One

"I wish to marry your daughter, if she'll have me." Her bewildered look of fear and excitement at his brash statement was one Mordimer would never forget. "I'm carrying four furs, twenty-two coppers, and eight silvers." At the word 'silvers,' the man's jaw went slack. "And if she'll walk with me tonight, I'll leave them all with you as a token of my good faith."

Indeed, Mordimer and Zarina left together that night. Navigating through the drunken depths of her father's greed, pride, and anger was not easy. The thought of freedom made Zarina's features sparkle with a whole new radiance, and Mordimer, emboldened by her looks of desperate enthusiasm, was prepared to win her at any cost. Much flattery, one threat, two rough exchanges, four furs, twenty-two coppers, and eight silvers later, the two walked quickly and awkwardly away from the swaying dock, not yet even knowing each other's names.

Sometimes Jastro transported people. Zarina's eyes narrowed the first time Mordimer described it to her. They had two small children now, a bigger room, and a growing secret stash of valuables from their years of hard work and modest living. Mordimer revered Jastro, he trusted him, and even though they rarely spoke, he believed Jastro to be an honorable man. The conditions of the voyage were not always clean and comfortable, and the passengers often looked bedraggled from their journey. *Who ever said sea voyage was easy?* he reasoned with Zarina. In truth, Jastro's tattooed crew dealt primarily with the passengers, who were often hurried into waiting carriages that trundled off into the narrow alleys of The Grotto, Rockmoor's southern borough by the coast. Mordimer just busied himself with the heavy traded goods, and decided at some point to stop talking to Zarina about the live cargo altogether.

His fingertips were bleeding now. The incessant searching and scratching, the hammering of his powerful arms on the heavy door and solid walls, were taking their toll. Zarina and the girls were reduced to soft whimpers and quiet sobs.

Suddenly, the door opened and light flooded in.

Mordimer rushed the intruder. He had rehearsed this moment in his mind all night long. *When the universe gives you a chance, you have to take it.* Just beyond the threshold were two people. The larger of the two he recognized. Mordimer's eyes grew wide in disbelief as he barreled forward toward him.

Even if he had not stuttered his steps in his moment of realization, Mordimer would have had no chance. In mid-flight, a flash burst from within the dark crimson robes of the second, smaller man, and Mordimer instantly lost control of his body. He sailed forward and out the door on momentum alone, and landed with a limp flop on the cold floor beyond. He heard the door slam behind him, but could not turn to look. He heard the impact of Zarina's body against it along with her anguished shrieks as rough hands grabbed him under his armpits and dragged him away.

Mordimer's lifeless body would not respond to his screaming nerves. He could see and hear. He could think, but he could not move. On they went, through a network of quiet stone passageways, his feet bumping noisily down short flights of stairs.

Chapter One

At last they stopped. This place was lit by several candles. There were books and parchments and countless jars. Working wordlessly, the two men stood him up in a tall box, and fastened him upright tightly with thick straps at his shoulders, waist and ankles. Before him on the floor lay an ornate rug. He had seen these rugs come off the trading vessels from time to time; Mordimer himself may have unloaded this very piece.

A low voice emanated from beneath the crimson hood. At the robed man's command, the big man who had dragged him here, the man he knew, knelt on the floor and slid the ornate rug away. Mordimer pleaded mutely for mercy with his eyes, but his former acquaintance was careful to keep his gaze averted.

Revealed beneath the rug, embedded in the stone itself, was an image resembling a black bat with ruby red eyes. Cold fear rolled over Mordimer.

The robed man was murmuring. He was hissing and grunting constantly now. He approached Mordimer's restrained and inert body and tore open the captive's tunic revealing the broad naked chest beneath.

Muttering louder now, the man placed a cold hand on Mordimer's heaving stomach. Mordimer's eyes roamed the room—dark things were here...skulls of animals and humans, beakers of what was most assuredly blood. And he could not be certain, but it seemed the ruby eyes in the floor were glowing now. They were *looking up at him.*

And now the robed man produced a long black serpentine blade. *Oh, god, no!* Mordimer screamed in his mind. He willed his thoughts—those that he knew would be his last—to his girls, and to his sweet Zarina.

This is it, he thought, *my last chance, and I had better take it.*

MORDIMER

With his mind nestled in that happy place, Mordimer's eyes saw his life's blood drain quickly from him in thick sheets onto the floor. Impossibly, his eyes saw the onyx inlay hungrily drink up every last drop, the rubies growing blindingly bright. Heavily drooping, his eyes saw the man in the crimson robes once more approach him over the clean dry floor. Finally his eyes closed and Mordimer saw no more.

Until several minutes later, when they fluttered open again.

But they were stark white now, absent pupils. The blank eyes that once belonged to Mordimer stared straight ahead unblinkingly.

"I'm gonna need to try it," Boudreaux mumbled, and then eyed the smith meaningfully through messy tangles of his thick brown hair. "You never know when a sticky situation might call for silver."

Chapter Two
BRIDGETON

"It's the perfect marriage of form and function, Boudreaux," whispered Arden intensely, holding up and examining another boot as though it was some precious ancient relic.

On his previous visits to this town, Arden had frequented the Bridgeton Armory but had never imagined he would be in a position to actually buy anything here. He loved the feel of fine, supple leather, he deeply enjoyed tastefully-colored and tailored garments, and he dreamed of well-fitted, light, strong, and flexible armor. But boots! Boots were far and away his favorite things, perhaps, in the entire world.

"I just love the long square toes!" he exclaimed. "I think these are the ones. They have the small steel-plate studding, the soft green reinforced snakeskin uppers, and the troll-hide soles. You should get a pair too, Boudreaux. Boudreaux?"

He'd lost Boudreaux. Somewhere between the third and fourth pair of boots, his massive companion had run out of patience and wandered away. Still holding his prize, Arden turned to see his friend across the room closely examining a fine silvery mesh tunic.

"Those pinch," he announced knowingly, as he threaded his way across the densely packed shop. "You're going to want silks underneath it, at least. But I think it would look really sharp on you, Boudreaux, plus it has good high neck coverage that'll really compliment that new helmet of yours. Which, by the way, you really need to have cleaned and polished."

Boudreaux grunted noncommittally, head still foggy from far too much ale the previous night.

"They do that here, you know." Arden was standing at his friend's side now. "Hey, feel the inside of this boot and tell me this isn't the most perfect piece of footwear you've ever laid eyes on."

Leaving the horror of the goblin lair behind them, the six companions had walked to Bridgeton as fast as their weary and hungry bodies would allow them.

That had turned out to be two days.

Shortly after emerging above ground, they had cleaned the blood and dirt from themselves, drank, and then filled their wine skins in the cold clear mountain stream. Hours later, at Gnome's encouragement, they made camp in a small forest just south of the desolated Westover. They had seen no living thing on their march, but after an hour or so of sniffing, crawling and waiting, Arden's superior outdoor senses enabled him to track and ensnare a small, skittish wild boar. X'andria sparked up a fire of dry leaves and slender fallen limbs, which soon roared brightly, and Boudreaux roasted their precious meal. As darkness fell, they were eating eagerly, and the only sounds in the night were the smacking of lips, the licking of fingers, and the crackling of the fire.

They slept in shifts with weapons at the ready, but thankfully the night had passed without incident. Setting out early the next morning under grey skies and light drizzle, they found themselves approaching Bridgeton just before noon.

"To the Dancing Deer!" exclaimed Boudreaux in an uncharacteristically bright tone.

"Lead the way, Boudreaux," sighed Gnome, with no better idea of his own. "They have rooms, right? Like the kind of rooms people can rent for more than an hour or two at a time?"

Oblivious to the jest, Boudreaux considered the question. "I don't know, Gnome. We'll ask Maddy when we get there."

To Boudreaux's sour disappointment, Mathilde, the bar maid at the Dancing Deer Inn, gave him a rotten look when he greeted her with the informal, slightly suggestive exuberance of an old special friend. Equally disdainful glances were cast by the few burly men standing at the bar.

Sensing trouble, Ohlen had stepped calmly forward. "Fair maiden, we six are weary from a long and arduous journey. We seek safe shelter and a hot meal, and are prepared to pay you well."

The difference was like night and day.

With Mathilde's good wishes and the promise of roast meat, stew, and fresh bread, they had soon headed up the narrow stairs, Boudreaux muttering dejectedly to himself as they walked. They had rented the largest of the inn's rooms. It was not quite spacious enough for them all to fit comfortably, but, ever cautious, Gnome insisted they stay together at least until they knew the lay of the land.

They had collapsed in exhaustion. Finally safe, with walls

surrounding them and civilization beyond, they allowed their mental and physical fatigue to overwhelm them.

The sun was still high in the sky, and Ruprecht and X'andria were still fast asleep, when a scrawny boy of no more than fifteen staggered into their room under the weight of an entire roast lamb on a wooden tray. Moments later he returned nervously with a cask of ale and six empty horns, and then skittered away without a word. Ohlen, Boudreaux, Arden, and Gnome ate and drank in silence, deep in their own tired thoughts. Soon only Boudreaux remained awake to finish the cask of ale all by himself. The others snored heavily, having fallen asleep without even clearing the mess from the tray, the floor, or from their fingers and chins.

"I'm gonna go buy more of those beautiful Bridgeton darts at the silversmith's," X'andria had enthused the following morning, fingering a small topaz from her stash of dwarf valuables. "Then I think I'll head to the gorge to see the bridge of Bridgeton—I've heard it's amazing. Does anyone want to come with me?"

"I'll go," came a staccato chorus of replies from Gnome and Arden followed closely by Boudreaux, who until that moment everyone thought was still asleep.

They had rested well. The good people of the Dancing Deer made an exhilarating morning brew of bark and needles and leafy herbs, served piping hot in small earthenware bowls, that helped prop open even Boudreaux's bleary eyes.

The silversmith's shop was part store and part museum. X'andria went straight to the velvet-lined tray displaying the large heavy darts of which she was so fond. The long, silver-barbed spears protruded fiercely from teardrop-shaped wooden bodies that gleamed from attentive polishing. The eagle feather flights were a study in balance and perfection.

"Oh, I just love them!" she gushed to the master smithy, and proudly showed him the wear and tear on the four darts still remaining in her possession. Reading a dark and cautionary look from Gnome, X'andria mentioned no goblins or demons, but instead claimed she valued her darts so highly that she recovered them on hunting trips whenever possible.

The smithy's eyes had widened when she produced her four scratched darts with squished feather flights from within her wrinkled and blood-stained night-blue robes, but he recovered his smile quickly and volunteered, "We can fix those right up for you if you like, young lady. Our commitment to the fine items we make here is life-long. If you have a few minutes, I'll get my apprentice to straighten and polish those so they're as good as new."

"Oh, could you?" X'andria was thrilled. To the shopkeeper's astounded surprise she added, "and I'd like to buy all the others here as well. I seem to be going through them a bit fast, you know?"

Boudreaux saved the smithy his reply by grunting, "This silver?" He had been closely examining an ornate short sword lying beneath a locked iron grate affixed to the floor.

The flustered smith addled over, handing off X'andria's four maimed darts to a short and powerful young man with dark smudges on his face who had appeared in the rear door of the shop. "Why, yes," he stammered. "That is a supreme weapon of pure silver over which I have labored for months. It is my masterpiece."

Boudreaux continued to study the blade.

"I'm gonna need to try it," he mumbled, and then eyed the smith meaningfully through messy tangles of his thick brown hair. "You never know when a sticky situation might call for silver."

The smith composed himself a bit, and replied, looking determinedly at the floor: "Look, I really appreciate your interest in our treasures, but I must advise you that the items we make here are extremely expensive, and," gesturing suggestively now at the four of them, all still clad in the torn and filthy garments they had worn out of the hideous goblin lair, "I'm just not sure this is the right shop for you all to be browsing."

At this remark, Boudreaux's expression contorted into something unpleasant along the lines of, *One more word out of you, and I'll tear your arms and legs off.*

Fortunately, Gnome interpreted this look before the shopkeeper did and stepped forward. "We apologize for our appearance, kind sir. We have been on a long journey. I am quite confident, though, that we can come to an arrangement you'll be very pleased with for the glorious missiles and the masterful blade."

"And this belt, too!" Arden burst in. "Just look at the setting of this opal—supreme craftsmanship!"

Flustered anew, the smithy looked down at Gnome and seemed to register the small character's presence for the first time.

"What'll it be for the darts, the sword... and the belt?" Gnome asked bluntly.

Gnome and the smithy fell to animated whispers as they negotiated a fair price for the items. The kindly man must have been convinced of their capacity to pay because when Boudreaux demanded loudly, "I need to handle the blade!" he jumped forward with keys in hand to open the iron cage containing the weapon.

A short while later, they left the shop, the owner beaming and waving behind them. X'andria carefully stowed her dozen new and four restored darts, Arden admired his attractive new belt, and Boudreaux glowered through half-closed eyelids, and slung his new silver short sword in a soft black scabbard over his back.

X'andria announced, "Gnome and I are heading to the gorge, you two."

Arden piped up, "Come with me to the armory, Boudreaux. We have *got* to get out of these smelly clothes." Boudreaux seemed conflicted, so Arden sweetened the deal: "If we go to the armory, Boudreaux, we can spar for a while afterward, before lunch."

The offer to spar was all Boudreaux needed to hear. He shifted his gait toward Arden and the armory, while Gnome and X'andria waved goodbye and headed in the opposite direction.

An hour later, the two men left the Bridgeton Armory wearing new boots (Boudreaux's were a bit more utilitarian than Arden's), new clothes, and for Boudreaux a new silver mesh tunic.

And an hour after that, they were sweating profusely in an open field, drilling thrusts, parries, and feints. Some children from the town looked on in amazement as their blades whirred and clashed. Boudreaux, a light breeze cooling his sweat-soaked face, found himself smiling for the first time since Mathilde had rudely rejected his advances at the Dancing Deer Inn the afternoon before.

The path led up to a great wooden bridge woven together with
thick ropes and fixed at either end to massive stone pylons.

Chapter Three
THE BRIDGE

The day was warm and clear. Gnome and X'andria walked along in pleasant silence through the quaint town. Ignoring a few stares from townsfolk who seemed unaccustomed to the appearance of a gnome walking alongside a young she-elf, they quickly found themselves at the southern edge of Bridgeton headed along a wide path into a thick, lush forest.

Gnome enjoyed being with X'andria. With others he was burdened with the impulse to assert himself. This was something carried over from his early years. When he had entered the world of Big People, it only made matters worse. His physical size and stature, and the speed with which he was written off as inconsequential, served to augment his insecurities.

Added to that was Gnome's fierce loyalty and tactical brilliance. Not only did he feel obligated to protect those he loved, he was also really good at it.

When taken together, these things kept Gnome in a relatively sour mood most of the time. His mind whirred with constant calculation, he braced perpetually for imaginary fights, and he dreamed up plausible consequences that would likely never come to pass, but clouded his consciousness nonetheless.

But all of the anxiety melted away when he was with X'andria. For some reason she put him completely at ease. Perhaps it was her easy-going demeanor—X'andria seemed wholly unconcerned with what other people thought of her. She was more interested in snails, flowers, and nettles than she was with speed, combat prowess, or dominance.

It also didn't hurt that, of all his friends, she was the closest to his size.

And then there was their shared obsession with magic.

"Did you ever do it before we met The Alchemist?" she asked, once they were a good ways into the wood.

"Sorry?" Gnome asked, "Do what, X'an?"

"Magic." She looked at him searchingly, her wide eyes like deep glassy pools.

"Oh my goodness," Gnome replied. "It was before we met, X'an, and it was totally by accident."

The gnomes lived in a deep and complex network of tunnels under a

series of rolling hills. While they had profitable relationships with a chosen few Big People whom certain members of the clan would meet above ground for trade, most would go for months or even years without seeing the sun.

Gnome was the second of two sons born to the eldest clan leader. From an early age, he was taught to fear and hate Big People, to fear and hate the sun. His early childhood was spent scavenging for edible roots, bugs, moles, and snakes, which he would deliver to his mother for use in stews and roasts. As he grew older, his father commanded that he practice knife fighting with his older brother, "in case their home was ever invaded by the Big People."

Gnome asked to see the outside world on many occasions. His requests were always met with stern rejection. His father would say, "Once you learn proper fear and respect of the world above, you may visit it." Logical even at a young age, Gnome countered one time, "But how am I to learn proper fear and respect if I cannot see it with my own eyes?" This bit of brilliance earned him swats about the ears and a night's stay in "The Hole."

Years earlier, the gnomes had tunneled too deep. They hit water in the depths, and with the water came cold, dampness, slime, and all manner of small slithery creatures. Rather than fill the tunnel, Gnome's father decided to seal it with a heavy oak door, and use it for punishment. He called it simply "The Hole."

What pushed Gnome over the edge, however, was when his older brother—who had never shown any interest in the world above—was chosen to accompany the lead trader to the surface to bargain with the Big People over the gnomes' fur garments, finely whittled woods, and polished gemstones. As he left to ascend toward the surface, he cast Gnome an arrogant smile normally reserved for those moments when he bested his younger brother in knife-fighting practice. Those *moments, incidentally, were now few and far between, since Gnome had grown to be quite a terror in close combat with the short blade.*

So Gnome snuck after them.

He crept behind his brother and the trader, against his father's explicit orders, and followed them all the way to the surface. He arrived in the open air and witnessed a spectacular sight that he would later come to know as sunset.

It took his breath away. Still stuck partially in the secret entrance to their home, with only his ears and head poking out, he stayed above ground just long enough to see the pink and orange fiery ball in the heavens dip behind the incomprehensibly vast horizon.

He would have watched longer, but he was snatched from beneath by his father, and dragged forcefully back inside. The beating and scolding he endured on the way back to The Hole was like no other he had ever experienced. His dad was in a towering rage, made worse by his embarrassment that his own son had defied his decree.

His father decided to make an example of him. Gnome stayed in The Hole for a long time. Occasionally his mother brought him food to eat, but he became so hungry in between meals that he even resorted to capturing and choking down some of the slithering creatures borne in by the frigid water at the base of the chamber.

That's when it first happened. He was dreaming about the sun, recalling the scene in all its glorious detail, when a large slimy bug crawled onto his hand.

Several things happened at once: his eyes flew open; his dad opened the door to The Hole to let him out; and he felt a surge of energy tear from his brain as the bug inexplicably burst into countless points of light, becoming a perfect shimmering replica of the sunset he had constructed in his mind.

"I don't think Dad had any idea what he was seeing or how it came to be," said Gnome, "but it was clear enough to him that I was obsessed with the outside."

Gnome concluded heavily, "So he told me, if I was so interested in the world above, that I should pack my things, leave them in peace, and never come back. The last I remember of them is my mother sobbing, my dad's arms crossed, and my brother's stupid grin. So that's the first time I did magic, and the last time I saw my family."

They walked in silence for a while. As they neared the sound of roaring water, X'andria knew instinctively she was the first person to whom Gnome had ever told his story.

"Thank you for sharing that with me, Gnome," she said in a small voice. "It sounds like a really tough journey you've had, and all I can say is," X'andria stopped to face him, her huge eyes glistening, "that I'm really glad you decided to come above ground, and that we found each other at Mama and Papa's."

They arrived at the gorge. It was magnificent. The path led up to a great wooden bridge woven together with thick ropes and fixed at either end to massive stone pylons.

"So much power," breathed X'andria. The rapid current of the wide and swollen stream rushed over the edge of an enormous waterfall, plunging into a pool at the bottom of the deep gorge far below.

They walked out to the middle of the bridge and stared over the edge for a long time. X'andria's mind raced as she imagined how someday she might learn to unlock nature's many secrets—to be able to control them. Gnome just drank in the beauty of the scene. He enjoyed the rare peace that the natural world brought to him, a peace he'd first known briefly when he saw that glorious sunset long ago.

"How about you, X'an?" Gnome asked on the walk back to town. "What's your story?"

As soon as he asked, though, Gnome wished he hadn't. X'andria's expression, normally so bright and open, became a mask of darkness. They walked for some time in silence before she finally spoke.

"I've never told anyone about it, Gnome."

"Please, X'an, forget I asked, alright?"

But she had made up her mind.

"You told me your story, Gnome, so I'll tell you mine." For her part, X'andria felt particularly comfortable around Gnome, too. With almost all men, she was aware of a certain degree of separation. The way they looked at her. The words they chose. The innuendo. There was often a thinly-veiled flirtatious desire mixed in with their actions. In Boudreaux's case, as much as she liked him, it was not veiled at all.

But with Gnome it was different.

Gnome was her companion and she always felt that what Gnome said, Gnome believed. Having Gnome as a friend was what she imagined having a brother might be like.

"I grew up far from here, across the sea, actually, in Atolia. Have you heard of it?"

Gnome nodded.

"I remember playing with the other elf children in these amazing green forests with crystal-clear streams and waterfalls. Not all that different than the gorge we just visited, except the elves knit things together with magic, not rope.

"I never knew my father, but thinking back I wonder if he left my mother when I was born, or if, maybe, the elves did not allow him to return to the forest and live with us because he was a man. I guess I'll never know.

"I don't know why my mom took me the night she did. She was fighting constantly with her parents. I don't think they ever really shouted, but I remember the tension between them, and I remember my mom crying most nights. So she was probably just trying to get away from them.

"She packed up everything she could carry, and we left that beautiful place in the middle of the night. We walked until morning. I had no idea where we were going. She didn't answer any of my questions—at least not that I can recall—but I do remember her singing softly to me. *Laamnu neila hiiwa.* Sleep little one.

"It seemed like we walked for days and days, but I'm sure it wasn't really that long. Eventually we neared the coast and the ground became sandy and the air became salty.

"She was so excited when we came upon the huge ship moored off the coast. And her excitement got me excited, too. It was all so new, and the air and the earth felt so hot and so different than anything I'd ever experienced.

"But it all went wrong. These huge painted men came toward us shouting in a language I couldn't understand. Mom was scared, I could tell. As soon as she realized they meant us harm, her body got all tight. It felt like stone, like she was heavy, sinking into the sand. She must have poured all her elf magic into the beach, because I remember the men sinking into it as they came at us. I remember the sand whipping their faces, knocking them down, trying to swallow them. But they were too strong, Gnome. They just kept coming. Mom fought so hard. She squeezed me so tightly, I remember it hurting—but for years after I would have given anything to feel her hold me like that again. I still find myself imagining it from time to time."

Chapter Three

Tears welled in X'andria's eyes, they welled in Gnome's too. After a few long moments she continued, "They finally snatched me away, and shoved Mom hard into the sand. I was so small, and they hoisted me into their huge sweaty arms and fought their way back toward the ship through mom's furious sandstorm. The last I recall of her, she was shrieking on that beach of swirling sand as they rowed me out to the huge ship. I could still hear her when they loaded me on board, and stuffed me below deck.

"Anyway. The boat was dreadful, so many prisoners stuck together. When we arrived in the city, I was made to carry water and food for the big fat man who owned the vessel, and owned me. Almost as soon as I got there, I started dreaming of escape. And eventually I did! It wasn't long after that, that I landed on the street and got scooped up by Mama and Papa. I still have nightmares sometimes about that boat and that terrible, fat man."

"I don't want to talk about it, Ohlen!" interrupted Ruprecht
with a shout, shaking now, and sweating a little.

Chapter Four
SEARCHING

"I just don't remember, Ohlen!" Ruprecht was whining now, clearly agitated and confused.

Ohlen was grateful the others had left the Dancing Deer Inn, giving him an opportunity to speak alone with Ruprecht. Ruprecht was back, yet in a sense, he was not. Since leaving the goblin lair behind, since the spiritual battle with darkness that had ejected the accursed orb from Ruprecht's body—but nearly cost Ohlen his life and his soul—Ruprecht had said almost nothing to anyone.

He wasn't right. Ohlen could feel it.

On the way to Bridgeton Ruprecht had trudged along behind the group, but it seemed that he followed only because he had nothing else to do. Almost as if he was biding his time. Ohlen alone had noticed the yearning that churned beneath his friend's calm facade. Given the malignance that Ruprecht had been exposed to, and pulled violently away from, yearning was particularly perilous.

"I know, Ruprecht. I know. I was there, too. You may not remember it, but I experienced some of what you did." Ohlen had a gift for reassuring and relaxing people.

"I'm sorry, Ohlen," Ruprecht blurted. "It's all just so strange, and I feel so guilty, like I did something terrible. And I don't even remember what it was. I'm just so sorry." He looked remorseful, like he might cry.

"It is really important for you to recognize that this was not your fault, Ruprecht. If the fault lies with anyone, it is with me. I am the one who dropped that horror and let it roll near to you," Ohlen said soothingly. "We have to realize that what is done is done. The important thing is that we all survived, and that you are back. But, Ruprecht, " Ohlen pressed on, "We also have to learn as much as we can from this, because I think we both know that it is not over. Whatever we encountered back there was just the tip of the rat's tail."

They sat silently for a long time, Ruprecht's expression inscrutable.

Then Ohlen ventured, "Do you remember the eyes?"

"I don't want to talk about it, Ohlen!" interrupted Ruprecht with a shout, shaking now, and sweating a little.

"Alright, Ruprecht. Alright. You listen, then, and I will share what I remember."

Blank stare.

"The first time I touched you after you had been invaded, it was like your body turned inside out and released a viper from some fathomless abyss. It was like the darkness itself formed into a body and assaulted my psyche. X'andria says I was actually knocked back through the air about twenty feet. All I know is that I went into shock, and when I finally woke up I had to struggle to rise above a penetrating blackness that had infected me."

Ruprecht was looking at Ohlen now, his lips slightly apart.

"I spent the rest of the time we were down there preparing for our second encounter. I prayed, I called upon the most pure and glorious powers I know, and I begged them to fortify me for battle.

"When we locked again, I met it, Ruprecht. My power allowed me to stay engaged past the initial onslaught of corporeal darkness. It talked to me, Ruprecht, it taunted me and laughed at me. It was awful."

A small amount of spittle had begun oozing from the left corner of Ruprecht's slack mouth.

"It promised me power, it showed me torturous scenes, it even showed me your mind and body wracked with agony. It threatened everyone we hold dear. And then ... and then I asked it to take me instead. I asked for the black orb to invade my body instead of yours."

Ohlen was sweating now, too, as the memory of the pain and struggle viscerally overcame him. Ruprecht was drooling and scowling covetously, eyebrows knit closely together.

"And it did. It swam into my brain and overtook me with a cruelty unimaginable to me now, even though I experienced it. My world was dismantled brick by brick. I fought with all my strength, but it just laughed at me. Those eyes: they mocked me, and smothered my will.

"I was almost entirely lost when something happened I cannot fully explain. This evil had decimated an entire clan of dwarves long before we arrived. On our way to find you, we stumbled upon their countless small corpses. Their spirits saved me, Ruprecht. It was amazing. It was like their martyred souls were waiting for an opportunity for vengeance, and through us, in the battle we were waging, they found their opportunity to act. They saved us both, Ruprecht."

It was a long time before either of them spoke. This time it was Ruprecht who broke the silence. "Do you really think, Ohlen, that it's not over?"

Ohlen did not reply. He did not like the glint in his friend's eyes one bit.

Master was releasing him. The straps loosened. The straps were gone. He dropped to a tense low crouch.

Find them. Stop at nothing. They are sealed. Like in a coffin. They are not far.

Hunt them. Smell them out. Tear everything apart. Bring them to Master.

With astonishing speed, what was once Mordimer slid and scooted like a huge hairless dog from the dim chamber.

Knocking over a table, two chairs, and very nearly several people, Boudreaux raced forward to embrace the squealing girl in a slippery, smelly hug.

Chapter Five
REUNITED

Sweating profusely, exhausted and thrilled, Boudreaux and Arden sheathed their weapons and locked their calloused hands together with an audible smack.

"Good show, my friend!" enthused Arden. "I haven't had that much fun in a long time. We must do this again, and often."

"Anytime, anywhere," panted Boudreaux, grinning his broad toothy grin.

The children watching them were gone now.

Approaching the Dancing Deer, with lunch on their minds, they spotted Gnome and X'andria ambling slowly toward them from the opposite direction.

"How was the bridge?" shouted Arden through cupped hands.

Chapter Five

Looking up from what seemed to be an intense conversation, X'andria waved enthusiastically and shouted back, "It was amazing! You have to go see it!"

Closer together now, Gnome added mischievously, "Yeah, you two could spar out on the bridge, see who falls in first."

Both Boudreaux and Arden privately considered this suggestion far more seriously than Gnome intended.

They entered the Dancing Deer together.

The inn was filled with people, all of whom bizarrely seemed to be expecting them. At their arrival, the dense crowd clapped loudly, cheering and smiling. The four friends surveyed the scene, flummoxed.

"Helga! My gods, it's you!" shouted Boudreaux ecstatically through the din.

Knocking over a table, two chairs, and very nearly several people, Boudreaux raced forward to embrace the squealing girl in a slippery, smelly hug.

"I can't believe it. I am so glad you got out. Oh my gods, it's so amazing!" he blathered. And the two of them fell to excited chatter.

Rowena stepped forward from the gaggle. Arden, tears mixing with sweat on his cheeks, could hardly believe his eyes.

A thin boy named Joseph raced over to Gnome. "It's you!" he cried, "I can't believe it's really you. I wasn't sure if I just dreamed you up, or if you really existed."

"Oh, I exist," Gnome replied bluntly, then—remembering Joseph's struggling gait to keep up with all the other fleeing prisoners in the goblin lair—he sweetened his reply, "And I'm sure glad you still exist, too, young man."

"I'll go get Ohlen and Ruprecht; they need to be here," whispered X'andria in Gnome's ear, and she vanished into the bustle.

"Ale!" Boudreaux was shouting, larger than life, when Ohlen, Ruprecht, and X'andria came back down the stairs.

A warm and raucous reunion commenced. While all parties did not know each other well, they had experienced a lifetime of terror and triumph together. The Westoveran prisoners had gotten out. They had made it to Bridgeton alive. Rowena had alerted the village elders to the tragedy of Westover and to the looming threat beyond. So when the starved and exhausted prisoners straggled into town, families had opened their doors, fed them, bathed them, and gave them shelter.

The children who had seen Boudreaux and Arden sparring in the field north of town had told their parents, and word spread quickly that the heroes had arrived.

"Ruprecht?" Rowena ventured, cautiously approaching the lone, cloaked figure sitting silently away from the group. He turned and regarded her as though looking across a wide expanse.

"It's me. Rowena, remember? You saved my life."

And something inside Ruprecht broke. He began to cry. They hugged each other for a long time. Rowena cried, too. Locked in that embrace, sobbing and swaying, they felt each other's warmth and life.

Boudreaux and Helga talked long into the night. Gnome was the first to notice that Mathilde now regarded Boudreaux with a whole new level of interest, and took special pains to refill his horn of ale whenever he needed it. And sometimes even when he didn't. Late in the evening, Boudreaux finally suggested to Helga that it was past his bedtime. He disappeared up the stairs, as did Mathilde, and neither was seen again until the following day.

Several blissful days passed in Bridgeton. There was much celebrating punctuated by a lot of work. The elders asked about the goblins in exhaustive detail. Their main concern, of course, was to know if they should expect resurgence. Ohlen and Gnome agreed that it was best to keep details about the demon statue and portal, if that is what it was, secret for now. But they freely described the location of the goblin lair, the complex of tunnels, the dwarf palace, and the enormous tentacular worm.

"We killed everything we saw," growled Boudreaux ominously at one point in the discussions, "but if I were you I would take more fighters than you think you'll need just in case any of the slimy bastards escaped our notice. Plus," he added wryly, "you'll need all the able bodies you can muster to haul back the loot we left behind."

Boudreaux scanned the eager faces before him, feeling satisfied with himself.

Fast as lightning, her left hand shot out from beneath her shawl and grasped the shivering chipmunk. She lifted it and painted its face with the muddy mixture.

Chapter Six
TOWARD ROCKMOOR

"But I don't see why you have to go at all," Helga persisted.

The smart, strong girl stood defiantly, eyes glistening.

"I'll come back and visit, Helga," Boudreaux replied in a voice so uncharacteristically gentle he surprised even himself. "Our path is taking us to Rockmoor, at least for now. And you and Rowena have a big job to do while we're gone. You must rebuild Westover. Your people need you to lead."

After much discussion, Ohlen had convinced the party of their need to strengthen and study in the wake of their mortal struggle beneath the mountain. They all agreed that Rockmoor would provide the tools each of them would need to learn.

So this final morning in Bridgeton, they gathered together in the

Chapter Six

Dancing Deer's taproom. It was bittersweet, as goodbyes tend to be.

"Hey," interjected Arden during a lull in the conversation, "I heard there is a mystical healer around here. Someone who might be able to help me with this?" He gestured at the part of his face, under his right eye, that had been melted by the mucousy tentacular worm they had faced in the goblin lair.

The villagers conferred briefly. Most had heard stories of a mysterious being who inhabited the deep woods to the east. The consensus described an ancient woman. None in the room had ever actually seen her, but they had all heard of a mythical pair of enormous oak trees that would present themselves as markers to travelers in need.

"We have something to say before we leave," Boudreaux announced. He and Arden exchanged a glance and stood up together. The chatter continued.

"Quiet!" Boudreaux shouted. He drew his dwarfish long sword and slammed the hilt, hard, on the heavy table in front of him. The humor had drained from his voice, and the talking ceased abruptly. Into this tense silence, Arden declared, "Westover must be rebuilt. It will be rebuilt with the treasure you uncover beneath the mountain." He eyed everyone standing around him, lingering especially on each of the young men, and continued, "We expect at least half of everything you find to be given freely to Helga and Rowena, here, for this noble purpose." Seated nearby, Helga straightened just a little taller.

Boudreaux concluded sternly, "Arden and I are gonna come back someday, and if on that day Westover doesn't stand, we'll find the misers responsible and make sure they pay in more than coin."

They were off.

The six friends had trekked several hours away from Bridgeton when Gnome recognized a pair of oak trees matching the village elder's description. As they came closer, Arden excitedly detected traces of foot traffic between them. Amazed they had actually come upon something resembling the tales of the mystical healer's dwelling, they left the road for the path between the two towering, vine-covered oaks.

The day was beautiful and bright, the breeze warm and gentle, but the thick canopy they were soon passing beneath made the space around them cool and dim. The path ahead looked even darker.

They walked a few minutes in silence, the way becoming gloomier with each step. "Who did you say this lady was, Arden?" asked Boudreaux, too loudly. Gnome, engrossed in the quiet assessment of the path before them, nearly jumped out of his skin. But in spite of the shushing, Boudreaux drove on skeptically, "What kind of creepy weirdo lives in a place like this?"

"Boudreaux, please keep these thoughts to yourself," Ohlen said in a careful low voice. "She is not far now."

They ventured on. As the path dropped steeply, so too did the temperature. Brambles, rotten logs, and leaves obscured the damp forest floor, and they were all grateful for Arden's intuition guiding them forward.

Myriad noises emanated from the ground around them and the trees above. Chirps and calls and shuffling and rustling sounded and echoed in the shadows. X'andria instinctively reached inside her robes for one of her darts, but stopped when she felt Ohlen's gentle and reassuring touch on her elbow.

"We have arrived," he announced softly.

They could hear a small stream trickling nearby. The forest noises had grown in intensity around them to a chorus of animal sounds blending seamlessly together.

Gnome's huge eyes drank in darkness as easily as light, and he was first to notice the low mound of mud and bracken that was the healer's dwelling.

"I see it," Gnome whispered.

"Will you come with me, Ohlen?" breathed Arden.

"Yeah, you're good at this kind of thing." Boudreaux, it seemed, was incapable of saying anything discreetly.

"We all go," Ohlen replied decisively. "Lead us, Gnome."

With their first step toward the mound, the forest went silent save for the trickling stream—as though all the plants and animals were holding their collective breath to see what would happen next.

Constructed as it was of mud, branches, and leaves, all manner of volunteer mosses and mushrooms had also taken root upon the mound. No obvious door greeted the friends; no light shone from within. Skirting the mound, Gnome noticed a slight depression in the hut's wall. The entrance, it turned out, was no more than a hole covered with a thick curtain of dark leafy vines.

As their party gaped, the thick vines rustled from within and a dim red glow spilled meekly out into the gloom. A wrinkled and hunched old woman held back the twisting leafy ropes with a gnarled hand and fixed them with a piercing gaze. She did not say anything. She did not beckon them forward. She did not smile. But she held the curtain open long enough that they felt obliged to enter. Gnome walked slowly into the candle-lit interior, followed by Ohlen, who smiled, stooped low, and disappeared inside.

"You two better go first," Boudreaux said to Ruprecht and X'andria, urging them forward. "We might take a while." Even leaving their bags outside, it proved awkward to get Arden, Boudreaux, and the heavy gear they wore, into the healer's home. Ultimately, they both crawled and slithered through the opening. To Gnome's consternation, Boudreaux took a fair amount of the old crone's hanging vines with him as he squeezed himself inside.

Eventually they found themselves sitting in a circle around the perimeter of the small round space. Three red candles flickered in the center of the room. They burned atop a tattered and dirty woven mat, and cast just enough shimmering light for X'andria to perceive runic script and mysterious images in faded earth tones.

The woman sat cross-legged. Slumped and covered in a grey shawl, with matted grey hair that obscured her face, she looked almost like a small mound of earth herself. Clay jars stood amongst small piles of powder, leaves, needles, and unknown substances arranged haphazardly around her, and a small striped chipmunk shivered by a wide and shallow bowl placed directly in front of her.

"Why have you come to visit Magda?" The raspy voice emanated from all around them at once as though initiating in the thick walls themselves. The mound that was Magda stayed motionless.

They all looked at Arden. Arden looked imploringly at Ohlen. Ohlen finally said, "One of our number has been injured, Magda. Word of your miraculous healing power has spread far and wide, and we have journeyed to see you this day to ask humbly that you might bestow your gifts upon him."

"Magda has no power," the walls wheezed, "Magda has no gifts."

Arden got a strained look on his scarred face as both Gnome and Boudreaux turned sharply toward him with narrowed eyes. X'andria was alternately fixated on the piles of components

45

surrounding Magda, and the wide basin before her. Ruprecht stared off into space.

"But Magda can ask the forest," she continued. At these words the chipmunk began bobbing rapidly up and down, and a shriveled hand emerged slowly from beneath the grey shawl. "The forest knows life and death, growth and decay. The trees and the earth may give a gift this day. Magda can only ask. Let the injured come forward."

Magda clawed messily in the piles around her. X'andria's eyes were huge. Without looking, or moving anything more than her one visible arm, the crone casually threw pinches of various ingredients into the basin before her.

Arden slid forward uncomfortably. Unable to stand upright in the shallow room, and not sure where to go, he just scooted toward Magda with his chin jutting out at an odd angle as though trying to come at the healer with the melted part of his face first. Boudreaux thought this looked hilarious, and even started to chuckle, until a threatening glare from Gnome helped him regain his composure.

A thin tendril of deep red smoke curled upward from Magda's basin. She was stirring her mixture now with the long nails of two stubby fingers. Fast as lightning, her left hand shot out from beneath her shawl and grasped the shivering chipmunk. She lifted it and painted its face with the muddy mixture. The lines she painted glowed a dull red.

The small creature raced to Gnome, who was closest, climbed quickly onto his shoulders, and briefly pressed the top of its head into the exposed flesh of Gnome's neck. This it repeated with each member of the party except for Arden who now sat before the basin, and before Magda. Magda, too, now had streaks glowing dully on her wrinkled face and forehead.

Gnome was the only one to feel rushing underneath them.

He had never felt anything like it, yet he knew with certainty what it was: roots. Roots slithered beneath them, probing forward through the earth like eels in a river. Magda, eyes closed, reached swiftly beyond her basin and clutched Arden's face at the precise moment that thin web-like roots burst through the earth all around him and snaked over his crossed legs.

All became silent and still. Curling reddish smoke began to fill the cramped space. It came from all of them now, and it glowed with a light of its own. Smoke seeped from the spots on their necks where the chipmunk had touched them. Smoke poured freely from the junction of Magda's hand and Arden's face. It all began swirling together like a dizzying blood red whirlpool.

Boudreaux snuck a glance around. X'andria was hungrily devouring every detail of Magda's rite. Gnome looked like he was going to be ill. Ohlen, eyes closed, was serene. Ruprecht wore an uncomfortable grimace, like he desperately wanted to be anywhere else.

"DESPAIR!" it was no longer just Magda's rasp, now a shrill chorus of accusatory screams filled the space as though borne on a gust of wind through a keyhole. The candles blew out. "You cannot win alone. You cannot run away. A dark storm comes for you. It comes for ALL!" Madness swirled around them. "Gather the light. Waste no time. Already the gaze burns us. The hatred scorches us. The darkness falls. Leave now! Run and take this evil terror with you. Magda will come to you when the fire rains and the battle rages."

An instant later, they sat blinking in the bright afternoon sunlight, sitting absurdly in a circle on the road, their provisions nearby.

Chapter Six

"What the hell was that?" griped Gnome as he rose and dusted himself off.

"That was amazing," X'andria exclaimed in wonderment.

"Sounds like nonsense to me," Boudreaux pouted. "Gather the light," he wheezed, mocking Magda's voice and waving his arms around to mimic swirling air. "Why don't we bottle our farts while we're at it? I've got a few stored up that I bet would be more useful in battle than a bunch of light."

"Hey, how's my face?" asked Arden hopefully.

They all looked.

"Still nasty and melted, man, sorry," Boudreaux returned sympathetically. Then, turning, he yelled indignantly at the forest, "Come on, lady, you didn't even fix Arden's face!"

They gathered their things and walked on for some time before Ohlen spoke.

"We are not strong enough," he stated simply.

"Speak for yourself, Ohlen," joked Boudreaux, flexing an enormous bicep and flashing his toothy smile.

"Quiet, meathead," said Gnome. "What do we do, Ohlen?"

"I am even more convinced that we must train, and learn, and improve. We must purify. And yes, Boudreaux, when the time is right, we must gather forces of light."

They had left the forest behind them now, and their trail dropped in elevation toward the sea. Around them waved the tall grasses of rolling hills. Dotting the landscape, huge rocky fingers thrust skyward.

"What did Magda mean by *dark storm*, Ohlen?" X'andria asked.

"I do not know for certain, X'andria. But this much seems clear. Some demonic shroud settled over the Westoveran mountains and brought destruction to dwarves and humans alike. It marshaled goblin forces, possessed men, and passed slaves through a mysterious gateway to another world. We came to Magda to ask for help to restore Arden's wounded face, and instead the powers of nature have given us a grave warning. A warning we must heed with the utmost care."

About three hours from Rockmoor, they stopped for a late lunch. Mathilde had sent them on their way with bread, meat, and cheese from the Dancing Deer, a jar of spicy pickled beets, and over Gnome's protestations, as much ale as Boudreaux could carry.

After lunch, Ohlen stood and made a most unwelcome announcement.

"Well, my friends. Here I must say goodbye." He was met with blank stares and shocked silence. The color drained from Ruprecht's face.

"Don't worry, I will catch up with you soon in Rockmoor!" Ohlen chuckled. "We all must become stronger in our own way. And my path forward is one of solitude."

They protested greatly, but Ohlen's mind was made up. The last they saw of him was his gleaming white-robed form striding purposefully over the crest of a sloping green hill to the south.

With the heaviness of determination, they turned eastward and set out on the final leg of their journey to Rockmoor.

*Like all cities, there were rich denizens and poor,
those who ruled, and those who served, those with greed
for even more, and those with ambition for advancement.*

Chapter Seven
THE MARKET

Gnome left their lodgings before first light. With bare feet he was almost completely noiseless, and with his dark cloak thrown over his thin, flexible leather tunic and trousers, his small frame was nearly impossible to detect in shadow.

And shadow is where he traveled.

Rockmoor was a port city with bustling commerce. Like all cities, there were rich denizens and poor, those who ruled, and those who served, those with greed for even more, and those with ambition for advancement. A few sought wealth by virtuous means, most operated with varying degrees of morality—and some just stole what they wanted outright.

Gnome threaded his way through the network of alleys behind

the long apartment buildings of the Westwood district. On the southwest side of Rockmoor, away from the coast, the mostly residential area took its name from the forest into which the neighborhood extended.

Nearly all the buildings in Westwood, including the rooms that he and the others had rented, were constructed of wide dark wooden boards harvested from the ancient forest. The best ships produced in Rockmoor were constructed of Westwood's finest oaks, and wide, elevated boardwalks formed the main neighborhood thoroughfares.

For Gnome, the boardwalks were perfect, because he was small enough to move freely beneath them. Wheeling around from behind a long, low tenement dwelling, Gnome dropped quickly into a small gap beneath the boards and raced along unseen toward the city center.

His destination was the fish and produce market just north of Westwood, on the south edge of Hillcrest. Morning markets in Rockmoor were always teeming with fresh-caught fish, and unwary Hillcrest consumers would most certainly be carrying coin.

These people will have something to steal, he calculated. *And I will be ready.*

One problem with running barefoot beneath the Westwood boardwalks was the rats. All manner of trash slipped and slid between the wide worn boards, and most of it seemed of interest to the huge grey scavengers. Rats were supposed to be nocturnal, but night reigned eternal in the dark beneath Westwood's elevated pedestrian streets. Their beady eyes regarded him fearlessly as he rushed by. Gnome was careful not to step too close, as these savages, raised on abundant quantities of discarded fish parts and refuse, had grown larger than any rodents he had ever seen.

Gnome skidded out from beneath the concealment of the boardwalk at the edge of the Torrent River. This wide, rushing river marked the border between Westwood and Hillcrest. Hopelessly polluted by human waste of all kinds, it continued east through the north end of The Grotto and the middle of Fish City before spilling its murky contents into Rockmoor Bay.

The low wooden walkway above him rose to become a bridge over the foul waterway. After a quick look around, Gnome scrambled up the nearest pylon and grasped the first girder of the rusty iron truss supporting the bridge's expanse. *Don't fall*, he thought grimly, as he swung deftly across.

Wood became stone and tile. Mosaic flourishes decorated even the most unlikely places in Hillcrest, which was home to Rockmoor's most affluent residents. As Gnome climbed to street level, easily scaling a tall foundation sunk deep into the riverbank, he passed a series of ornate mosaic roses placed in a line just above ground level. *Mine are some of the only eyes that will ever notice these*, he reflected sourly. *This is the kind of waste that happens when people have too much money and too little sense.* Gnome did not care for Hillcrest.

He slowed his pace. The sun was just rising now, and he was at street level. His senses prickled as he slid noiselessly from alley to archway, shadow within shadow.

Even at this early hour, the market was bustling with purveyors of all kinds. Hillcrest was quite a distance yet from Fish City and the Bay, but sea smells clouded the air. Wheeled carts carried all manner of salty carcasses along with the reek of room temperature watery death. Gnome detested water and did not trust anything that lived in it. He had grown to tolerate his friends' taste for fish, but the pungent odor of the market caused him to wonder anew how anyone in their right mind could find the smell anything but repulsive.

A large stand tended by a round sleepy woman showcased beets and potatoes, radishes, cabbages, and green leafy bunches. *Now this is more like it*, thought Gnome as he slid quickly between the rear of the stall and the high stone wall that bordered the whole market square. A quick appraisal told him that in the unlikely event that the big woman or anyone else came looking behind the stall, the space beneath it would provide adequate cover for him to crawl away unnoticed.

There he waited.

The early bird shoppers arrived. Ironically they were always the most alert, the fiercest negotiators, and the most difficult to steal from. No thief with good sense would attempt to pilfer from them. Even so, Gnome almost immediately spotted what he had ventured out to find.

His target was young. *Almost my size*, thought Gnome. As Gnome watched, the adolescent perused the stands casually but did not touch anything. He was easily missed and thoroughly forgettable. *An amateur with potential*, Gnome appraised.

And then it happened, fast as lightning, and gentle as a breeze: the slightest contact, darting fingers, and the small thief separated some precious thing from its wealthy and oblivious Hillcrest owner.

Now for the hard part.

The thief was on the move. Having acquired something of value, he had to disappear before the mark realized anything was amiss. The small thief darted quickly into an alleyway that led east from the square. Gnome departed the obscurity of his hiding place, and ran briskly around the market's perimeter in pursuit.

He makes too much noise, scolded Gnome in his mind, as he followed the soft padding footsteps into the gloom. Soon the clean stone facades gave way to clay and thatch structures with rounded corners and eroding walls. The worn dirt pathways had muddy blotches here and there most likely made by drunks and scoundrels too coarse or too witless to walk to the Torrent to urinate.

The thief was heading into The Grotto.

He's pretty fast for a little guy, Gnome thought wryly, as he glided noiselessly at a safe distance behind. The boy knew routes between buildings, under bridges, around open roads, and through a wide underground sewer that kept him out of sight. They crossed the Lower Torrent River on a makeshift footpath beneath a bridge and headed into the heart of The Grotto.

There were no real trees here, but the muddy streets and densely-packed, dilapidated buildings sagged and crumbled into an overgrown park of sorts that was constructed of vines on top of vines on top of shrubs and what might once have been man-made structures since pulled down and smothered by time. The occasional iron fence, or mound of dark brown wall, could be glimpsed beneath thick curtains of woven green.

Gnome's quarry disappeared. The boy had raced along, rounded a corner, and promptly evaporated. This could mean only one of two things: either The Den was near, or the hunter had become the hunted.

"Hmm, I dunno." The creep called Rove feigned consideration.
"Should we let Boris squish you, little man?"

Chapter Eight
THIEVES

Shadow was becoming harder to find. With every minute, the sun crept higher in the sky, illuminating the pitted dirt road and causing the peculiar green smell of dense foliage to mingle with the muddy odors of The Grotto and the foul, ever-present wafts from Fish City. Bugs of all kinds had awoken in the thicket, and their buzzing seemed loud to Gnome in the absence of other sounds.

He walked slowly and warily along the narrow road, the backs of low clay hovels on his right, the buzzing expanse of green undulating to his left.

Where on earth did he go?

Several things then happened in quick succession. A shifting shadow caught Gnome's eye from within a darkened entrance on his right. In front of him, perhaps forty paces away, a small section of the road seemed to settle slightly, as though an earthen trap door that had been open a crack was suddenly closed. Focused as he was on the road and the buildings, Gnome never expected the enormous hand that closed over his face, suffocating him and pulling him aggressively backward against a huge, soft body. A massive hairy arm closed quickly over Gnome's torso, pinning his arms hopelessly to his sides. Blind and immobilized, he felt himself being hauled backward directly into the thicket. Buzzing and heavy breathing filled his ears.

After a disorienting and bumpy descent, he was deposited unceremoniously, but unharmed, on a dirt floor. Dim light in the shabby underground space illuminated a ring of cruel blades wielded menacingly by a motley bunch of scoundrels. Taking a quick look behind him, Gnome saw that the enormous man who had apprehended him was twice the size of the next largest person in the cramped space. He had to stoop low to avoid hitting his enormous head. While everyone else leered accusingly at Gnome as if waiting for the moment when they could skin him alive, the giant man just stood there, smiling like a child who has caught his first fish.

"You got followed, Waif," a wiry man hissed admonishingly through broken teeth. Regaining his bearings, Gnome recognized the small thief whom he had pursued cowering silently by a wall.

"I thought 'e was just a boy!" blurted out a dirty, skinny girl enthusiastically.

"Ugliest boy I've ever seen," retorted the wiry man.

"What are you, anyway?" a tremulous voice entered the conversation over Gnome's left shoulder.

"I'm Gnome," said Gnome.

"Fig didn't ask *who* y'are, he asked *what* y'are," spat back the wiry creep.

Gnome responded with his most withering glare.

"Should I squish 'im, Rove?" rumbled the huge hairy oaf behind Gnome. Somehow his voice sounded perfectly amiable even when threatening murderous violence.

"Hmm, I dunno." The creep called Rove feigned consideration. "Should we let Boris squish you, little man?"

In defiance of the hovering blades, Gnome stood up purposely, dusted himself off, and stated, "I am here to see The Master."

Those were the magic words. The blades drooped. A combination of relief and disappointment played out on the eager faces surrounding him. Several scoundrels just walked wordlessly away, presumably to resume whatever activity they had previously been engaged with.

Rove, still glowering suspiciously, spat sideways at the huddled young thief by the wall. "Why don't 'e follow you to The Master, Waif? You let 'im come with you here to The Den, why not take 'im all the way? An' you can tell The Master all about how you led 'im here while yer at it."

Departing the dank space on the heels of the shaky young thief, Gnome projected his purest disdain at the taunting wiry Rove. His gaze was met by hatred and a barely contained fury; Gnome knew this man could never be trusted.

"You're a good rogue, Waif," Gnome said sincerely as they threaded their way lower into the earth through a series of twisting passages. "You were hard to follow, and you lost me at the end."

They entered a stone-lined room. A single blue candle burned on a wooden table filled with valuables of various kinds. An ornately carved and generously upholstered chair sat empty and slightly askew just behind the table.

Waif crept to the table and extracted a silver bracelet with a single topaz cabochon set in the center from a pocket inside his tattered grey cloak. He placed it carefully atop a small pile of coins, trying not to make a sound. *So that's what he stole in Hillcrest*, thought Gnome.

The voice came from the shadows only after Waif had attempted to slink back out of the room. "You have something to tell me, Waif." The soft words rang clear and emotionless.

Waif froze. His features gained the pained distortion of a boy trying very hard not to cry. "I'm s-sorry, Master!" he blurted out in exasperation. "I got followed. I led him to The Den. I was careless. I'm so stupid." The words tumbled alongside the tears and the guilt and the shame.

"Everything happens for a reason, Waif." Still no emotion whatsoever. "I will see you soon, and we will proceed."

"Yes, Master." Waif bowed and vanished.

The space was so quiet now that the burning of the candle became the loudest sound in the room. With the candle's dim light, even his superior eyesight failed to provide Gnome with The Master's location in the subterranean blackness beyond the glow. The Master's voice had seemed to jump around the room.

"Why have you come?"

Suddenly the voice was so close behind him that Gnome whirled around. He saw a compact figure straighten up after landing silently and feather-light on the floor. Had he leapt from some perch in the darkness above? Intense, coal-black eyes bore down into Gnome's. They peered out from a clean, inscrutable face, framed by curls of thick black hair.

"Master," Gnome bowed low, "I am here to learn."

With each passing day, their tactics improved,
their speed grew, their endurance increased.

Chapter Nine
TRAINING

"What's the deal with Ruprecht?" Boudreaux asked gruffly as he and Arden clomped along the boardwalk toward the forest at the edge of Westwood.

The training grounds were not far from their lodgings. Just as soon as Boudreaux woke up each morning and doused his face in cold water, the pair set out together for long days of physical conditioning, target practice, and swordplay.

"Ruprecht," Arden paused. This was a difficult subject for him. "It's hard to explain, Boudreaux, you never knew him when he was... normal."

Since their arrival in Rockmoor, Ruprecht had been largely uncommunicative. For two days he had not gone outside at all. That was worrisome. Then on the third day they had come home to find Gnome and X'andria wondering aloud where Ruprecht could have gone. He had not returned for two full days. That was even more worrisome.

"The thing is," Arden continued earnestly, "Ruprecht used to be such an amazing man. He was so strong and yet so kind at the same time. And he had an incredible gift. Do you remember that dwarf pool that restored you and Ohlen and that poor guy Geoffrey? Somehow Ruprecht, with the help of the gods, was able to fix people like that with just his hands. It's just so terrible what happened." Arden trailed off. "I wish you could have known him before."

"Me, too," sighed Boudreaux heavily, "because the guy I see now scares the hell out of me."

Arden looked at Boudreaux quizzically. *Scared* was not a word he had heard pass Boudreaux's lips before.

"I know, I know," Boudreaux hastened. "I just don't trust him, and yet here we are, all sleeping in the same room together each night." He took a few more heavy steps and then added stonily, "Usually when I don't trust something, I kill it."

Arden liked Rockmoor. They had found their lodgings in Westwood quickly, and immediately set about following Ohlen's advice to improve their skills and strengths. Westwood was particularly perfect for Arden because not only were the training grounds nearby, but so, too, was the Westwood Forest.

Gnome was gone each morning before anyone else even woke up. He snuck out at odd times in the evenings as well. He did not talk about where he was going or what he was doing, but otherwise he acted just like the same old Gnome. On the third day Arden pressed him about how he was spending his time. Gnome got a very serious look on his face, said something about "The Code," and changed the subject.

X'andria was generally the last to rise, the last to leave, and the last to come home at night. When the rest of them fell asleep, her candle was still flickering, her nose buried deep in one of her books. Her mouth would move as she silently shaped the words she was reading.

The boardwalk ended at the forest. Arden and Boudreaux jumped to the ground, hardware jangling as they landed heavily on the earth. Boudreaux felt the familiar and welcome pulse of adrenaline at the mere thought of the exertion in store for them. He lived for this.

On the edge of the forest, the training grounds consisted of a lodge, a field, a sand pit, a shallow pond, and an archery range. By day's end, Arden and Boudreaux would have spent ample time in each.

Fast, precise, intuitive, and deadly, Arden was lethal with one blade or two. These days he concentrated mostly on his skill with two. Defending against his relentless spinning steel, times two, was fantastic practice for Boudreaux. Arden was also a superior shot with a bow. Generally disdainful of missile weapons, Boudreaux had now been on the receiving end enough times to be convinced of their utility, and agreed to learn some of the tricks of the trade.

Boudreaux was impossibly strong. Arden felt himself almost

constantly kept off balance, because if Boudreaux landed even one direct hit, the day was over. While Arden's speed greatly exceeded Boudreaux's, Boudreaux's sheer power allowed him to defend adequately even when his footwork was not always completely synchronized. On the field they were well-matched, but in sand or in water, Boudreaux's phenomenal power gave him an advantage that almost always ended with Arden lying face down, gasping for breath, his friend laughing and offering a hand to help him back up.

Both of them enjoyed the training immensely. With each passing day, their tactics improved, their speed grew, their endurance increased, and the number of people watching them doubled.

"Want a drink?" Boudreaux asked hopefully, once they had finished their last grueling practice in the pond. They had taken to ending in the water, to rinse off some of the sweat and blood, and to help cool down a bit.

Boudreaux already knew the answer, though.

"No, I think I'll walk in the trees tonight, my friend." Arden already had the far away look in his eyes that took over whenever he was preparing for his sojourns in the woods. "You feel like a walk?" he asked politely, though they both knew he really wished to be alone with nature for a while.

"Honestly? I feel like a bottomless horn of ale and the warm company of whichever lass serves it to me." Boudreaux laughed heartily as he stood and walked in the direction of town.

The forest was alive. Whenever Arden entered, his senses were instantly overloaded with the abundant vibrancy of the natural world. It was like he could see with his nose and ears as well as his eyes. Everything around him told a story: the slight rustling in the underbrush as a rabbit sought shelter; the faintest trails in the leaves and needles betraying a squirrel's comings and goings; even bird droppings hinted at dwellings, vantage points, safety, peril.

On Arden walked, smelling and listening, experiencing the story of another glorious day in the miraculous forest. Then he came upon something for which he had no explanation.

Animals in nature did not ruin things. Even bears would not break limbs off small trees just to pass through. No creature, not even a wounded one, would scrape along the earth leaving divots in its wake. And no normal being would, by its passing alone, create a dead zone through which none other dared tread.

But that is precisely what Arden found.

For anyone else, the scene may have been overlooked or merely puzzling. Another might have noticed the destruction and assumed, perhaps, big animals had fought and caused some damage that nature would repair in time.

But not Arden—his blood ran cold. The senselessly veering path. The total disregard for life. The monstrous power, the recklessness, and the lifeless void left behind. Arden stepped warily backward, his pulse pounding in his ears.

This night, the forest had told a deeply troubling tale.

X'andria met Elias each afternoon, and they had decided he
would teach her how to move objects with her mind.

Chapter Ten
THE EMPORIUM

"Breathe, X'andria. You have to remember to breathe," Elias reminded her persistently.

The great tome hovering several feet above the table came crashing down, and X'andria let out a gasp of frustration.

"It's so hard," she complained. "When I seize it with my mind, it takes all my concentration just to keep it there, and it feels like I'll lose it if I do anything else."

"Which is why you're going to practice it again, right now," Elias said patiently. "Because here's the thing, X'andria. You know how you were describing the crushing feeling you get when you levitate? Like the weight of the object is pushing directly down onto your brain? What you're feeling is the force of the energy you have gathered pressing on your mind." He spoke more deliberately now, "Air is the only thing that dilutes that power, X'andria. If you are going to practice without pain, get stronger, and survive the focus of even greater power, you have got to master your breath."

The Emporium was located in Watertown, the seaside district between Hillcrest and the coast. Almost anything could be found in Watertown. Home to Rockmoor's sailors, not only was there a constant influx of exotic goods, there was also a voracious appetite for all manner of food, drink, and entertainment. The largely transient population brought rich talent, diverse taste, and a particular disregard for decency. The sailors and thrill-seekers coexisted in lukewarm symbiosis with the merchants and barkeeps who bought and sold the visitors' wares each day and filled their cups each night.

There were shops with furniture or furs or hardware of all kinds. But sometimes cargo came off the ships in the dead of night that was not for general consumption. Sometimes these items were too precious or too powerful, or too dark and nefarious for the light of day. And when treasures arrived that possessed abilities of their own, with personalities and desires embedded in them by their makers or bestowed upon them by magical beings, the cloaked sensates of The Emporium would materialize out of mist and shadow on the docks and make persuasive offers on behalf of the Sorcerer of Rockmoor.

The Emporium was famous. Even situated down an alley off a side street in Watertown, intrepid tourists and curious kids would stumble upon it from time to time in hopes of witnessing something miraculous or of altering their minds more dramatically than the dull and fuzzy escape that came with draining horns of ale in the seaside taverns.

And they would find both of those diversions at The Emporium.

When, on her second day in Rockmoor, X'andria first pushed through the doors of the small dimly-lit shop, she saw two young men giggling over a stick on a shelf that would hiss at them like a snake any time they reached for it. An older woman with sagging, red-rimmed eyes and tangled grey hair leaned heavily on a counter, behind which a bored-looking dark-featured man absentmindedly paged through a large book. A vial of electric-green liquid stood half-drunk in front of the woman, and X'andria could see many more just like it for sale on the shelf behind the attendant.

Disappointed by the whole shabby scene, and ready to turn around and walk back to Westwood, X'andria's sharp eyes halted over the illusion. In the back corner of the shop, an empty table and the wall behind it were only *half there*. Her eyes saw them, but her mind did not. It was a strange duality she had experienced before when witnessing Gnome's phantasms. A lesser intellect would not even register the distinction, but X'andria's powerful cognitive reasoning overcame the spell.

Still standing just inside the shop, she glanced again at the clerk behind the counter. He gave her the slightest of nods, before returning to the book that lay open in front of him.

So she slid past the young men, now fully absorbed in watching a mechanical dragon stalk jauntily around its wire cage, and she slipped unnoticed straight through the table and the wall into the space beyond.

Books.

She arrived in a network of cozy rooms featuring gorgeous and ancient-looking polished wooden floors, exotic and ornate carpets, and couches and chairs of all kinds. There were several people strewn throughout the space, in various states of slouch, each of whom glanced up as she entered, but none greeted her or looked away for long from whatever they were studying. While each room had a different feel, all had floor-to-ceiling shelves filled completely with books.

Wandering from room to room, it was several minutes before X'andria came to her senses, closed her slack mouth, and swallowed the saliva that had liberally accumulated with the total immersion of her imagination. Glancing about nervously to make sure no one would chastise her, she randomly chose a medium-sized book with a faded green binding and sat down to read.

Twelve hours passed before she looked up again, hunger clawing weakly at the edge of her consciousness. She was dimly aware that others had come and gone, but none had spoken to her. In fact, she did not think anyone in the entire space had said a single word all day long.

It was a magnificent feeling, being surrounded by knowledge and wisdom stored in countless volumes. She had only made it a few rooms deep into what she now realized was a vast labyrinth of connected chambers yet to be explored. At the end of that first marvelous day, she gingerly placed her green book back on the shelf where she had found it. Her head was swimming with the precise details of alchemical preparation: the drying times and storage procedures for roots versus leaves; the diets to feed toads, lizards, rats, bats and creatures she had never even heard of, before harvesting their organs, eyes, claws, and tails for purposes she could only imagine.

She was stepping slowly back toward the invisible portal to the shop-front and the banal world beyond, when she noticed a tall blonde man exiting purposely across the room before her. More precisely, she noticed he was leaving with two books tucked under his arm. X'andria froze! *Could it be permissible?* she wondered, barely daring to hope.

In a moment of brazen courage, she retreated back to the shelf that held her precious green book, retrieved it swiftly, and walked briskly from the marvelous rooms with sweat beading on her scalp, feeling like the whole world was watching her. *I'll bring you back tomorrow,* she thought, as she cradled her prize and stepped out into the moonlight over Watertown.

X'andria passed several glorious days in The Emporium's library, from which she came and went freely, devouring as much information as she could. At first she went about it randomly, pulling whichever book struck her fancy, and curling up with it for hours on end. The third day, however, she walked slowly around the five rooms comprising the library and began to recognize categories like Materials—from which her little green book had come—Techniques, Theories, Runes, Potions, Scrolls, Memoirs, and Worship.

There were many books she could not read because the language was unrecognizable, and some books simply would not allow themselves to be removed from the shelves. One large black volume with a red symbol painted in slashes on its worn cover, gave her a massive headache the instant she opened it. She slammed the tome closed and then teetered back across the room to return it to the shelf.

It was in the middle of that third day that she looked up to see the tall blonde man for the second time. She noticed his high black boots first, because they strode into the field of her peripheral vision and stayed there. When she finally looked up, she was surprised to find that he was gazing back at her, a curious smile playing on his lips.

"Do I know you?" he said.

"I don't think so," X'andria whispered self-consciously—several people had lifted their heads at the sound of their voices. "But I saw you here a few days ago." She paused awkwardly and added in all sincerity, "I don't think we're supposed to talk in here."

He chuckled softly and replied knowingly, "No, I suppose we're not. But listen, my name is Elias and I am going back to Practicum. If you get to a good stopping point," he gestured past the next room, "come back and say hi."

Then he was gone.

X'andria tried valiantly to concentrate on her runes for several minutes, but it was no use. Somewhere between intrigued and annoyed, she eventually stood up and ventured beyond the final room of the library, to find what Elias had referred to as "Practicum."

Four days had passed since then.

Practicum, it turned out, was a honeycomb of nestled narrow spaces in which practitioners could try out techniques with relative privacy. At his invitation, X'andria met Elias each afternoon, and they had decided he would teach her how to move objects with her mind. Since The Alchemist, Elias was the most intriguingly knowledgeable person she'd come across.

Breathe, she kept telling herself. *Here we go.*

Levitating an object required compressing the power latent in the atmosphere all around her and forcing it to obey her command. To do so, she held a small loop of gold wire that conducted her will into the ether. Elias, it seemed, was able to do this easily, and he demonstrated the technique repeatedly for her while breathing noisily in and out and holding his eyes open wide.

X'andria had always focused best with her eyes closed. Her eyelids and brows squished tightly together, her lips pursed, and her diaphragm seized, she would pour all her concentration into focusing her will.

But according to Elias all that had to change.

"I don't care if it doesn't even lift off the table, X'andria," Elias was pressing. "At this point, it is more important that you relax, keep your eyes open, and breathe, than if the book even twitches." Elias, X'andria had learned, could be quite moody, and at this moment a bit of frustration tinged his words.

"Alright, Elias, I'm trying as hard as I can," she retorted.

X'andria breathed slowly. As she drew together her power, she resisted her natural inclination to close her eyes. She became aware that her shoulders were tensing and hunching, so she relaxed them. It was odd, actually. X'andria sensed the elements responding to her will, yet she felt like she wasn't really working that hard to make it happen. She imagined the book rising from the table.

The book popped into the air. *Breathe, X'andria.* This was way too easy! She could see it, too, because her eyes were open. She spun it several times, the pages flopping open and closed as it rotated. Breathing steadily now, X'andria realized she had made an enormous breakthrough.

It's not as hard as I thought it was.

She pulled the book toward her in the air. She positioned it in front of her face, and she willed the cover to open.

It hovered there, open to page one, for about two seconds and then crashed unbidden to the floor. But the plunge did not result from any error X'andria had made on her own; it came about because Elias had reached out and placed his hands on her shoulders. The unexpected shock of his touch had been the surprise that caused her concentration to fail.

"You are just extraordinary," he was purring as she whirled incredulously around to face him. Her first emotion was anger. She did not like being touched without warning, and she was mad at being interrupted just as she was beginning to succeed. But as soon as she saw him peering down at her, she was reminded that his guidance had brought her to this next level, and that she ought to be thankful.

Elias casually floated the book to its original position on the table with a flick of his fingers.

"What really excites you, X'andria?" He looked at her with an odd expression that she could not quite place, and, for the first time, she noticed dark circles beneath his eyes. "What do you want more than anything?"

The anger drained. His question caught her totally off guard. Her nature was to plunge fully into any mental challenge laid before her, and this question presented a new challenge indeed. *What do I want more than anything?*

"You know what I want, Elias?" she said firmly after some time. Elias leaned closer. "Fire." Her eyes were shining now. "I saw a man pour jets of white hot fire from his fingertips and turn it..."

"Hush, X'andria!" Elias interrupted with a conspiratorial whisper, and looked all around them as though expecting the very walls to come alive.

Composing himself quickly he continued in a normal voice, "It's a beautiful day for a walk, isn't it? What say you and I get some fresh air down by the sea?"

They led him, wide-eyed, into the clean opulence of Hillcrest,
to the massive white temple that would become his home.

Chapter Eleven
DORTMUND

Dortmund worked harder than anyone else.

Living, as he did, in the bowels of the temple, he studied feverishly by dim candlelight. The priests favored him, he knew, because of his intelligence and skill and utter devotion. That was why they chose him to live in the temple, and entrusted him with the sacred duties of caring for the grounds, the sanctum, and the crypt.

Dortmund's father had been a sailor. He never knew his mom, but he understood from his father's stories that she was an ungrateful wretch whose stupidity was exceeded only by her gluttony. On land,

Chapter Eleven

Dortmund's dad was perpetually drunk and prone to fits of violent rage that caused the pale, skittish boy to hide under whichever piece of furniture was least broken. When he was beaten, he would escape in his mind to a world in which he was supremely powerful. It was a world where others did his bidding. It was a world he continued to visit long after his father's death at the hands of another drunken sailor on the docks one muggy summer night.

The Brothers of the faith discovered him begging for scraps on a dirty street in Fish City at the north end of The Grotto. It was shortly after his tenth birthday, and they led him, wide-eyed, into the clean opulence of Hillcrest, to the massive white temple that would become his home.

Prayer and devotion consumed his life. He knelt for hours in his scratchy burlap pullover with the other orphans. He made a point of starting earlier and staying later than all the others, because he overheard one of the priests whispering one day about the importance of total commitment.

But the prayers did not make sense to Dortmund. They told him to clear his mind, and his mind would not clear. They told him to welcome in the spirit, and the spirit did not come. They told him to be penitent before God and he found himself, instead, wandering back to the world where he himself was God, and the rest of the inhabitants were prostrate before him.

There were miracles. Dortmund witnessed things that set his young mind afire. One night he saw a man carried hurriedly into the temple bleeding copiously from a huge gash across his chest. Ashen and barely conscious, he was carried to the center of the sanctum and laid on the marble floor, blood pooling around him. Four of the Brothers rushed to his aid, placing their hands on him and bowing their heads as Dortmund was ushered from the room to join the other boys for bedtime.

Dortmund awoke early the next morning, and stole from bed without waking anyone. Intrigued by the bloody scene of the night before, he secretly wanted to see the wounded man one more time to feed his own growing guilty obsession with violence.

When he entered the sanctum, he saw that the kneeling brothers had not moved one inch. Heart pounding, Dortmund crept quietly up behind them and peeked between their rigid bodies for a glimpse of the gore his adolescent brain so desperately craved. What he saw, however, was unexpected and even more thrilling than he'd imagined. Dry blood still caked the man's chest and the floor, but the wound was knitted closed and he was breathing normally. By their prayers alone, the brothers had put his body back together!

Dortmund smiled inwardly as he was dragged away for rule-breaking and flogged. When the lashes bit into his backside, he slipped easily away into his dream world where his subjects feared his might and praised his mercy whenever he deigned to heal the wounds that he himself had caused.

After that episode, Dortmund redoubled his efforts to appear pious. He made faces of ecstasy during prayer, paused longer than the others in reflection after lessons, and crunched together his jet-black eyebrows in sincerity any time the Brothers addressed him.

The happiest day of his life was when he traded his shapeless burlap pullover for a brown robe of the brotherhood and they informed him that his clerical studies would begin. That same day he was also granted access to the temple library. While pure devotion was something that he found frustratingly elusive, the acquisition of knowledge was a matter of dogged persistence—Dortmund excelled at doggedness.

Several confusing years passed during which Dortmund did

everything he could to learn and succeed, while the Brothers grew increasingly impatient with his total failure to commune with their deity. After a particularly trying episode, Dortmund was sent to see one of the priests.

He dragged his heels to the inner chambers.

Dortmund did not understand why, but he knew he was failing. He knew they were asking him for one thing, yet, try as he might, he seemed to be delivering great quantities of something else. As he neared the small arched doorway past the Sanctum, he imagined walking through his own great castle. Pushing inside, he saw his subjects before him, frowning because they secretly wished to be as great and powerful as he.

In the inner chambers, the Brothers said words to him. They offered to him the job of *groundskeeper*, and in his imaginary world Dortmund heard *ruler of the kingdom*.

He readily accepted.

One benefit of being groundskeeper was access to nearly all parts of the temple. Each night Dortmund hungrily studied the darkest and most depraved of the temple's books. The more he read, the more his imagination was fueled by fiery desire.

Some nights he even snuck into the crypt. His favorite book described rites of sacrifice and invocation that called for all manner of components including human and animal remains. Rationalized in some deep dark part of his mind, Dortmund desecrated the tombs in the dead of night to steal teeth and skulls and bones. These he added to a growing stash of dark objects hidden beneath the floor in the black basement where he lived.

DORTMUND

Five years passed.

Dortmund was outside picking up sticks when he saw a pallid face peering through the bushes at the edge of the temple grounds. This was a new one. He approached the bushes cautiously, but when he arrived, the face—and whoever it belonged to—had disappeared.

Was it a spy? Dortmund walked around to the back of the huge temple, to the entrance of his basement dwelling, whistling loudly and cracking sticks as he went. He slammed the wide door over the dark descending steps as if he was going within. But he was not inside. *No he wasn't*—Dortmund was only making it seem that way. Instead he crept stealthily around the far side of the bright white temple. He slithered through the bushes at the border of the grounds, ignoring the puzzled stares of nearby pedestrians. He stalked around the perimeter, careful to stay low and hidden, and he looked for the interloper.

Dortmund did not have to search for long. Across the wide street—in the shadow of an alleyway—the spy was hiding, face upturned at the shining temple as though studying every detail. Racing across the street, Dortmund grabbed the arm of the startled mystery man and coughed out, "Gotcha!"

The man's eyes went wild, like an animal caught in a trap. Dortmund had dreams of dominance, but he also desperately craved companionship. In the terrified eyes before him, he saw the potential for both.

"I'm Dortmund," he said, now catching his breath.

"Ruprecht," the startled guest managed, as he meekly tugged his arm free.

*Clandestine arrivals required flawless
nighttime navigation, and perfect silence.*

Chapter Twelve
THE DOCKS

Jastro's trading vessel swayed and creaked as it cut its way through the gently undulating night-black water. The big man had spent more of his life on the sea than on land, and while in his early years he had dreamed of amassing enough wealth to retire on one of the many islands he had visited, he now knew that the sea was too much a part of him ever to let it go.

Fortune had smiled on Jastro. Luck found its way to him on the wings of shrewd decisions, quick wit, and ruthless savagery, in equal measure. As dim lights winked like low-slung stars from the docks of Rockmoor, Jastro reflected on his current predicament.

I hate him. He realized grimly. *I hate him, I want him dead, and I*

Chapter Twelve

don't even know his name.

Long ago Jastro had smuggled his first slaves into Rockmoor. He had pangs of guilt, but he justified his actions, telling himself they were mostly being sold to wealthy magistrates in the high-walled compounds of Hillcrest. The slaves would have difficult lives, but they would stay relatively safe, and they would be fed, so long as they did their jobs faithfully.

Some were destined for darker fates, but that, Jastro reasoned, was their business. It was up to each individual to pull him or herself up to better circumstances. That is, after all, what he had done just as soon as he was bold enough to thrust that harpoon into his own master's back, and help him overboard, sputtering and cursing, all those years ago.

But this was different. This man was evil. Jastro knew that the wretched souls he delivered to this sadist would all die terrible deaths. And yet he felt he had no choice. Two weeks earlier, Jastro had seen things he wished he could unsee: a premonition of the wrath that would soon be unleashed. He knew when to fight, when to run, and when to build an alliance. With his own hide on the line, there'd been no real decision to make.

Right on cue, he became aware of moaning below deck. This would not do. Clandestine arrivals required flawless nighttime navigation, and perfect silence. Jastro jerked his head in the direction of the secret hold and barked an order to one of his hulking Islanders, who stood alertly nearby monitoring the bay.

The enormous man nodded slowly, and removed his loose white tunic to reveal a jacked torso covered in swirling tattoos. He walked starboard to a pile of fruit-filled crates and began sliding them several feet forward. When the last crate was moved, it revealed a coin-sized hole in the deck into which he inserted a thick finger. Grunting more from habit than actual effort, he hoisted the removable trap door concealed in the deck and looked down at six huddled men and women suddenly illuminated by the moonlight.

"Quiet," he growled, his accent so thick it sounded as if his tongue was at war with his throat.

Jastro smiled and looked serenely ahead as an orange and green glow danced on the deck behind him. A terrified gasp issued from the prisoners, but no more noises came from the hold for the rest of the voyage.

As the dock drew near, his Islanders sprang into silent action. Two of them flew through the air like acrobats and landed on the dock. Coiled ropes were thrown expertly from the ship to the waiting deck hands, and the ship was quickly moored.

Rats.

Jastro heaved his big frame onto the makeshift steps placed hastily on the dock beneath him. The rats were everywhere. But they weren't behaving like rats. They were not foraging and they did not scatter when he stepped toward them. Jastro's mood soured further.

"Did you have to bring *them*?" he hissed into the night.

"Dark times call for extra caution, Jastro," came the low response, just a few feet from his face.

And now he saw it. A faint rippling was barely visible in space itself, like the dark water beyond had been painted perfectly on flowing fabric and suspended right in front of him, blending with scintillating perfection into the background.

Standing further away in the darkness were three figures: two small ones behind a large man Jastro knew to be an Islander formerly in his employ.

"Do you have the Atolians?" the faceless low voice rumbled, menace never far beneath the surface.

Chapter Twelve

"Do sharks swim in the sea?" Jastro retorted dryly, and flicked his hand absently in the direction of his ship. Two of his Islanders melted out of the night and moved to retrieve the prisoners.

"And I will need two more of your *assistants*," the voice pressed on aggressively with no hint of compromise.

Jastro was accustomed to getting his way. In most cases he approached negotiations playing the jovial and magnanimous merchant of the world. He found that laughter and generosity disarmed his targets, and made them pliable as he communicated his velvet-cloaked demands. But with time and trade came inevitable disagreements, and Jastro occasionally found utility in threats of force. Rarer still had been those few critical moments when Jastro was pushed to cruel violence by the need to establish his dominance. In those moments Jastro was capable of a white-hot fury that blinded all other judgment and enabled him to overwhelm even his fiercest adversaries.

At this unexpected demand, blind rage boiled between Jastro's ears. Fury exploded within him at the thought of losing two more of his precious Islanders to this cretin, not to mention that poor sod Mordimer. Muscles twitching in his face and neck, it took every ounce of his self-control to stuff his anger back down along with the bile rising in his stomach.

He was saved from having to respond verbally by the appearance of the six bedraggled prisoners on the deck above. With all the efficiency of many years' loading and unloading cargo, Jastro's massive Islanders whisked the frightened Atolians down to the dock.

Then came the shriek.

Darting forward from the shadows bustled the two smaller men. But they were not really men. Unclothed, they were covered instead by grey fur. Black eyes glistened hatefully above open protrusions in their faces that were lined with pointy teeth of varying sizes. Their horrifying unnatural visage caused one of the prisoners to scream uncontrollably. They hastened to the sorry huddled human mass with alarming speed, silenced the noise, and began aggressively herding them away with oversized hairy hands, the fingers of which ended in curved black claws.

The rats on the dock swarmed behind them in a roiling grey wave.

The only thing left for Jastro to do was to be graceful about his defeat.

"How about these two?" he said with forced cordiality. The two members of his crew nearest him looked on coolly, betraying no emotion.

"They'll do," was the icy response. "Don't stray far, Jastro."

He absentmindedly pulled back his robe from his left arm to show the scarred mutilation left behind by the sphere's whirring blades.

Chapter Thirteen
DARK CORRIDORS

They looked at each other for a long time in that alleyway, not sure of what to say next. Something in Dortmund's manner put quiet, ruined Ruprecht at ease. Feeling at ease around another person was a welcome change indeed. For Dortmund, Ruprecht's obvious anxiety and confusion were like delicious confections for his starved ego to gobble up.

"Are you," Ruprecht stammered at last, "in The Brotherhood?"

"Oh yes, Ruprecht," replied Dortmund without hesitation. "The temple is mine, actually, would you like to see where I live?"

The lie was so easy, Dortmund believed it himself.

With no alternative in mind, Ruprecht conceded to be led across

Chapter Thirteen

the street, through the bushes bordering the temple grounds, and around the back of the great structure to Dortmund's basement stairs.

"Very few people are allowed in here, Ruprecht," Dortmund said with gravity. "I hope you know how special this is." And he bent over and pulled open the large flat wooden pallet that covered the dark stone steps winding down into the space beneath the temple.

Being underground again felt good to Ruprecht. As soon as they left the daylight behind them, he had a strong sense that he just wanted to stay here in the darkness forever. Dortmund lit a stubby candle and held one hand in front to protect the flame as they wound through a network of damp narrow passages.

"I like this place very much," Ruprecht spoke for the first time since leaving the alley. His voice was stronger now. "Lately I've had a little trouble knowing exactly who I am and what I want, but here I feel clearer, more centered."

They had reached Dortmund's chamber. He used his little candle to light several large lanterns, and soon the flickering flames set the space aglow.

The room was densely packed but very orderly and clean. Stacks of books sat on Dortmund's table. On the highest one perched a human skull. There were several earthenware jugs, and an array of cruel-looking iron implements that might have served surgical purposes. A woven rug covered the center of the ancient stone floor, around which waited several simple and sturdy wooden stools.

"Tell me about yourself," began Dortmund awkwardly.

Ruprecht studied the rug at his feet, and replied, "As I said, I'm not altogether sure of much these days. Maybe you should go first."

"Very well," said Dortmund, eager to spin his tale. "Here we do all the things you'd expect. We shelter orphans, train those who take the sacrament and show great promise, heal the sick, and give hope to the masses. The usual stuff." He paused to lick his lips, "but I have developed further interests of my own. Passions, you might say. Having learned the healing arts, I have decided to become a master of..." he was searching for the right words, "I have begun to master greater powers."

Ruprecht did not know what Dortmund meant by "greater powers," but he was feeling more and more at home with each passing moment. His new friend's casual demeanor caused Ruprecht to feel as though he could say anything without enduring the judgmental reproach of Gnome, the disapproval of Boudreaux, or the pity projected upon him by X'andria and Ohlen. Of all his old companions, Arden seemed the most accepting, but even Arden's searching gaze made Ruprecht feel guilty just for being himself.

"I don't remember much," he blurted, as if in a trance, "but I've been told what happened by others and so I have begun piecing it all together in my mind."

Dortmund held his pale, pock-marked face motionless in attention.

"There were five of us in a cabin in the forest. Ohlen found a little black orb, like a marble, that he said was the most powerful thing he had ever seen. We invaded a goblin hoard to free villagers who'd been taken captive, and Ohlen dropped the marble by accident after taking an arrow in the shoulder. I was kneeling just a few feet away."

Ruprecht was droning on in a monotone, totally unaware that Dortmund's shoulders were hunching now, his back arched almost like a hound raising its hackles.

"The orb hit my hand." He absentmindedly pulled back his robe from his left arm to show the scarred mutilation left behind by the sphere's whirring blades. "It grew these barbs that swam inside my hand. It invaded my body and there was nothing anyone could do to stop it. Hurt so badly. But it was thrilling at the same time."

Tears were welling now in Dortmund's wide eyes. A gnawing hunger awoke deep within him, and his pulse became deafening in his ears.

"I felt so much power." Ruprecht paused as though trying to recreate the feeling, even if only for a moment. "In a flash, I saw fire and ice, blinding light and total darkness. I experienced the most unbelievable bliss stoked hot by the torment and suffering of countless souls. It's like I was feasting on their pain. And I wanted more, I deserved so much more. I was so close to having it all." His maimed hand reached outward into the dim room and grasped the thin air in front of him.

Dortmund was standing now, leaning forward, as if he thought he might be able to experience what Ruprecht was describing if only he could get close enough.

Ruprecht seemed to snap out of it. "Anyway, everything just seems so bland now, Dortmund. I'm so confused. Every part of my body craves that power and ecstasy, yet I know the suffering I caused is wrong. It's terrible. I know that. I just... there's just a loud voice inside my head that simply doesn't care."

Suddenly Ruprecht felt exhausted. The weight he had been carrying had finally been lifted. He sat silently for a few seconds, Dortmund hovering above him like a spider waiting for the right moment to ensnare its prey.

"Ruprecht," Dortmund rasped, his tone saturated with lust and desperation, "where is it now?" He moistened his pallid lips again, "Where is the orb now, Ruprecht?"

When she arrived at the docks the next day, she walked confidently up to her new teacher, gave him a wink, and said, "I got it," before stealthily returning his precious parchment back to the inside of his robes.

Chapter Fourteen
PRIVATE LESSONS

The look in Elias' eyes told X'andria that she ought not mention the conjuration of fire anymore within the walls of The Emporium.

"It is a beautiful day," she agreed, a little too loudly for the small Practicum space they were in, but effective, she felt, for any imaginary ears that might be eavesdropping on their conversation.

"Well then," Elias smiled and suavely offered his arm, "shall we?"

X'andria managed a smile in return, but chose to fill both her arms with the books she had borrowed from the library.

"That is quite a story you were telling me, X'andria," Elias said in a hushed voice once they were a safe distance from The Emporium. They headed east toward the coast, the docks, and Fish City. "What exactly did you see? It sounds fascinating."

Chapter Fourteen

"Oh, it was incredible, Elias," she whispered back, looking over her shoulder—Elias' cautious behavior was infectious. "The fire just poured out of his fingertips in these roaring jets, and then it all swirled together over his head in a ball that got bigger and bigger and hotter and hotter." X'andria was more animated now, as she recalled the vivid memory. "Then he flung it straight at us. But a strange man we'd met—Geoffrey, I think his name was—created some kind of magic wall, and the huge ball of fire hit the wall and spread out in every direction like it wanted to get through to incinerate us. It's like the fire was alive, Elias!"

Elias had stopped walking abruptly and turned to face her. His expression was an odd combination of intrigue and, perhaps, longing.

"Oh, I know it sounds unbelievable," she scrambled. "I was a little woozy and I'm not sure I really have it all exactly right. But that is pretty close to what I remember, and Elias," X'andria leveled a sober stare straight into his dark-rimmed eyes, "I'm dying to know how it works."

She couldn't tell if he was sad, or thoughtful, or angry. Her story had definitely affected him deeply, and it seemed he was trying to choose his words carefully. They had resumed walking by the time he replied.

"I guess I'm just concerned for you, X'andria. If what you say is true, and I believe it is, it seems to me like you could have been in serious danger." They were at the docks now, and Elias was looking out to sea as if he might find the right sentiment floating somewhere amongst the waves. Finally he continued, "I really like you, X'andria, and I just want you to be safe."

Elias' worry annoyed X'andria slightly, but she waited politely before replying, in a somber tone that seemed to echo his concern, "Thank you Elias. Seriously. But I'll be alright. I've taken care of myself this far. One thing I have learned, though, is that there is much more knowledge out there. And don't you think the more I understand, the safer I'm likely to be?"

More steps, more lapping waves, creaking docks and pungent smells. "There are powers," Elias began darkly, "powers greater than we can imagine." He spoke with new resolve now, as though he had made an important decision. "I will teach you what I know, X'andria, but we must never speak of this in The Emporium. In fact, it might be better if we stop seeing each other there altogether. Let's meet here, at the docks, at midday tomorrow, and we can begin."

"Elias is just incredible!" X'andria enthused. Boudreaux and Arden were lounging in their small Westwood dwelling when she got in later that night. "He's going to teach me starting tomorrow, I'm so excited."

The two men traded glances over the top of their ales.

"What?" X'andria demanded defensively. "What was that look for?"

"Nothing, X'andria," Arden recovered quickly, "That's really great that he's going to teach you. What are you hoping to learn?"

"Well, I'm *so* glad you asked." X'andria sat upright now, her eyes gleaming. "First let me show you what he already taught me."

"This might actually be good," Boudreaux mumbled to Arden under his breath, his eyebrows raised suggestively, as X'andria fumbled for her small loop of gold wire.

Breathing slowly, and fixing her stare, X'andria focused first on her presence in the room, the energy in the space around her, and the energy in the air surrounding their cottage. Next she focused on Boudreaux's horn of ale.

"Hey!" the big man sputtered as his ale floated quickly from his grasp and into hers. X'andria took a big gulp of the bubbly golden brew and let out a breathy, "Ahhhh."

"I think I hate this guy," Boudreaux pouted.

"You don't even know him, Boudreaux. Elias is really nice, he's super smart, and I think I will really learn a lot from him."

"Come on, X'andria," Boudreaux retorted, "Do you really think for a minute that he has anything on his mind other than getting his magic little fingers inside that bodice of yours?"

This, it turned out, was not the right thing to say. Not only was X'andria clearly furious, but her feelings were hurt as well.

Arden tried to mend things. "Boudreaux is just concerned for you, that's all."

For his part, Boudreaux stood and stalked across the room to find another horn to fill.

"Not all men think the way you do, Boudreaux," X'andria fumed.

"Oh, I think you'll find that they do, X'andria." Boudreaux tried to strike a note of sincerity, "It's just that not all men are honest about it."

Thankfully they were both gone when she awoke the next morning. Ruprecht must have come back after she fell asleep, because he was snoring loudly as she prepared her breakfast. She gave him a long, sorrowful look before leaving quietly for the docks.

"I don't have long today, X'andria." Elias looked more exhausted than ever and was all business when she approached him. "But I have brought you something very special, very powerful, and very secret. Before I give it to you, you have to promise me a few things."

"Of course, Elias," she said earnestly.

"Promise me that you will take this straight home, that you will not bring it within the walls of The Emporium, and that you will show it to no one."

"I promise," X'andria intoned solemnly.

"I want you to read and memorize every rune and symbol on this parchment tonight." Elias continued, "Return it to me here, this time tomorrow, and our lessons will commence." And with that, Elias produced a thick roll of parchment and stuffed it quickly within her robes, as though sunlight might damage it, and then he turned and strode swiftly away.

Elias was not able to meet every day, but each meeting brought with it a revelation for X'andria. The scroll he had given her was a study of elemental fire. She had raced back to their cottage and poured over it like a child with a new favorite toy. She read the lines, and then closed her eyes and said them over and over in her head from memory. There were lists of critical components like wood or ash or flint or air, but the bulk of the treatise consisted of theories about how a focused mind might supply those elements from the ether if they were not physically present.

X'andria excelled at learning. When she focused, her mind could soak up complex details, and lock even the most intricate images into vivid memory. When she arrived at the docks the next day, she

Chapter Fourteen

walked confidently up to her new teacher, gave him a wink, and said, "I got it," before stealthily returning his precious parchment back to the inside of his robes.

They began with sparks. He assembled small piles of dry parchment, or leaves, or wood, and taught her, always breathing, eyes always open, shoulders always relaxed, to ignite the fuel with her thought alone.

After a few days wherein she lived and breathed and dreamed the invocation of flame, he presented her with a small silk bag that housed a piece of flint, a small square of parchment, and a pinch of ash.

Elias' fingers were strong and surprisingly scarred and calloused. He and X'andria sat facing the sea on a rocky outcropping between two huge docks. He had grasped her hands in his, and was describing the precise form her fingers needed to take, the sensations she should expect, how she needed to hold her hands away from her body and point her palms away from anything flammable, so that nothing unexpected would catch fire the first time she called it forth.

Uncharacteristically, X'andria's focus was drifting away from the content of Elias' lesson, and came to rest instead on Elias himself. She was listening more to the rhythmic low rumble of his voice than to the words he was saying.

And she was enjoying herself immensely.

"Try it now," he requested perfunctorily. Elias looked more and more drained each time she saw him. While his knowledge was vast, he had a demanding and sometimes harsh teaching style. His blue eyes, slightly bloodshot today, searched her green ones from just a few inches away.

"Alright, Elias," she heard herself saying, and she elevated her hands before her, palms skyward.

"Wait," Elias injected, "X'andria, you need to have the components in one hand."

"Oh, of course!" she laughed. And she fished out the little silk bag and held it loosely in her left hand while extending her right. She looked intently at the space above her right palm. Then she involuntarily looked past the space at movement on the dock beyond.

And she froze.

"X'andria?" came Elias' voice, echoing distantly as if from another world.

X'andria flashed back to her childhood. She was a little girl. She had dropped the tray with the cheeses. They were going to beat her and lock her up. She was hiding under the table. She was so scared she was trembling. She was completely powerless. She missed her mom so badly it ached inside her.

Her brain felt like it was overfilled with hot, heavy blood. Full to bursting. But her heart kept pumping more in. It felt like her ears were filling with blood. Like any moment, blood would pour from her nose and mouth.

"I know you're scared, X'andria, but get over it, alright? I don't have all day." The distant voice impatiently scraped at the surface of her consciousness somewhere far away.

The man was enormous. He stalked toward them along the dock. He was menacing, a long, curved scimitar strapped to his waist. He came closer. But what terrified X'andria were the tattoos. She would recognize those tattoos anywhere. How could she ever forget? How could it be possible that *they* were here?

In a fog, X'andria rose shakily to her feet. Heedless of Elias' now insistent pleading, she stumbled backward up the rocky bank and ran blindly away as fast as her legs would carry her.

As soon as Elias was old enough, his mother Estela
had begun transferring knowledge to her son.

Chapter Fifteen
ELIAS

Elias' earliest clear memory was of the chill morning air and lush green vista that greeted his blue eyes when he stood on tiptoe to peer through the balistraria in the highest turret of Ingroff castle.

His early boyhood had been spent in gloomy candlelit chambers and dark narrow corridors, but some part of him knew instinctually that there was more to the world—to get there meant going up stairs.

As soon as he could walk, he took every opportunity to trundle away and explore the feel and taste of anything he could grab hold of. *How his mother would yell at him.* He had no idea, of course, that many of the objects surrounding him were dangerous or even deadly.

Stairs were his favorite. There was a set of inviting steps that beckoned him in the open corridor off the chamber in which he and his mom resided. Putting his pudgy little hands two steps up, twisting and placing the inside of his bare knee on the first step, and hoisting himself upward, was pure thrill. He rarely got very far, though, before the air would close around him and he would sail backward, limbs flailing, to land unceremoniously at his mother's feet.

It seemed she was always mixing things. Mixing things or reading, with her thin lips barely moving as she processed the words. When he landed sprawling at her feet, she would admonish him crossly without even looking up from her work.

His mom frequently went through the Big Door on the other side of the room. When his mom went through the Big Door, Maud would watch him, standing with her hands on her hips, or sitting and sewing, but always with the sourest of expressions. Maud was quick to whack Elias if he misbehaved or tried to go exploring. She never took her eyes off of him, the way his mom occasionally did. So he learned to behave whenever Maud was around.

But the Big Door opened by itself one day, and a huge man in a scary black mask rushed in. He wore studded black leather pants, but no shirt. Instead, a patchwork of scars peeked through mats of thick dark hair that swirled around his flabby chest and belly. He was shouting something Elias did not understand, and his mom raced out of the room without so much as a glance behind her. The heavy door slammed shut, and Elias found himself completely alone.

There were so many steps. More than he could have imagined existed in the whole world. And after he finished with one set, he discovered another around a corner not far away. Laboriously taking one at a time, he rose higher and higher, the air changed, the light changed, and the boy grinned with eagerness for more.

It was all worth it.

The effort of the ascent, the swift punishment and the stricter rules that followed, were nothing compared to those few glorious moments looking through the slit in the thick stone walls at the world beyond. The sight would fuel his ambitious imagination for years to come.

As he grew up Elias came to understand who Carlton and Bertrand Ingroff were, and the role his mother played in their precarious rule over the Southern Plains. Privileged boys, the Ingroffs spent their adolescent years toying with swords and bows, avoiding their lessons, and chasing after the daughters of their father's subjects.

Their father, Theodor, was not a generous man, but he had a combination of basic decency and dim wits that led slowly to the erosion of the Ingroff fortune. When the old man died, the spoiled boys, now young men, found themselves with deteriorating coffers and increasing irrelevance throughout the plains. They had inherited their father's dim wits, but had not one ounce of his decency. Instead they had lavish tastes, and one fateful night, they set a course that would bring misery to the region for years to come.

Estela was a powerful witch.

Snatched as a girl by the self-proclaimed *Southern Sorcerer*, she grew up watching cheap tricks of light and smoke dazzle villagers who, so distracted, missed the real magic trick: their disappearing wallets. As soon as she was old enough, Leopold the *Southern*

Chapter Fifteen

Sorcerer took her for his bride. But it was no wedding of mutual consent, love, or commitment.

Instead, her wedding went like this:

They had made camp near the beach. The old man had taken to getting drunk after each show, and he had begun to hold her close to his foul, sunken body when he slept. His breath was rancid, and she hated being near him in every way. Luckily he would pass out quickly, and she could push out and away from his bony clinging grasp.

One night Estela decided to kill Leopold the Southern Sorcerer. He had stolen her from her family, made her roam the countryside with him, and lately had forced her to share his stale breath at night. She visualized the murder clearly. She crept quietly away from him and located the hunting knife he kept in a leather bag on his push-cart. Fierce resolve in her eyes, she stalked back to his wheezing, snoring body and braced herself to draw the big blade deeply across his jowl.

But her plan did not unfold the way she hoped.

With the knife inches from him, his body simply disappeared. This was a far better trick than the cheap charlatanism he usually trotted out for the townspeople they stole from night after night. Instantly trembling, Estela dropped the blade, which stuck in the earth and wavered accusingly at her feet. She looked fearfully around her.

Leopold was floating upright, about five feet away, hovering in a bluish light. He looked younger somehow: more vibrant, more powerful. In spite of herself, Estela found herself actually drawn to him for the first time since her abduction.

He did not yell at her. He was not even frowning. He said many things before the light dimmed and he sunk back to the ground. But the only one she could remember was, "If you're old enough to murder me, Estela, then you are old enough to marry me."

In the dim moonlight he strode toward her. The hunting blade leapt from the earth into his outstretched hand. Without hesitation he drew a deep crimson line in his left arm that dripped all over her when he reached for her to do the same. She screamed and squirmed as the blade bit, but his grip was like iron. He was muttering now. He dropped the knife back to the ground and pulled powders and bits of mysterious things from his robe and sprinkled them on her oozing wound one at a time. Smoke and sparks issued from her sliced arm as he added things and muttered louder and louder and finally, he pressed his own wound to hers.

Estela never stopped hating Leopold. But in that moment she came to understand him, and their spirits were locked together in that loveless, bloody marriage. She came to know that, whatever rite he had forced upon her, took away her ability ever to harm him again.

But two good things came from their marriage. The first was his knowledge. He freely and eagerly taught her everything he knew. He was a fountain of wisdom, and though he lacked drive and ambition, and was far too fond of mead and ale, he had impressive powers and a desire to pass along his skill.

The second good thing to come from their marriage, about five years later, was Elias.

Estela and Leopold began performing together, and their travels took them to the Southern Plains. They performed at Ingroff Castle at the invitation of two princes, and gave an impressive display of exploding lights, fire in the shape of great serpents, and chairs animated to walk all by themselves.

But the brothers, Carlton in particular, were far more enchanted by Estela than by the magic tricks she and the *Southern Sorcerer* had cast for their enjoyment. The performers were invited to stay the night in the castle. After much revelry and mead had put Leopold in a dazed stupor, Estela was offered a tour of the grounds.

"Kill him," she said simply. "Kill him, and I and my power are yours." Blood-red powdery smoke puffed faintly from her eyes and nose as she spoke.

The Southern Plains were slipping away from the Ingroffs' dominion. The brothers had just been hoping for a little entertainment this night, but what they got instead was so much more.

She saw the hunger reflected in their eyes. She saw how desperate they were, how helpless. "The people are deserting you," she said, trying not to betray how desperate her own situation truly was. "They are worshipping their own gods, trading their wares, looking away from their old allegiances."

Estela rose dramatically from the ground in a bluish glowing light; Leopold had taught her that one, too. "Kill him for me, and I will help you bring the flock back to its shepherds."

The bond transferred that night. It trickled down the shaft of Bertrand's sword, out of Leopold's shocked and convulsing body, and snaked its way into Bertrand instead. And through all the blood and agony of the years to come, all the torment and torture of the purging of the plains, Estela stayed by the Ingroff brothers as their faithful servant, strategist, and sorceress.

As soon as Elias was old enough, his mother Estela had begun transferring knowledge to her son. He had learned to recognize parts of plants and animals, and became expert in the drying, cooking, extracting, and distilling of components of all kinds. By this time, of course, he knew what was happening behind the Big Door. The anguished screams, that earlier he had accepted as just part of the world around him were now intelligible to him, and he knew that they belonged to the *terrible* men and women who had betrayed the benevolent princes of Ingroff Castle and who worshipped false gods.

Only once did Elias witness his mom create a being from dead material. A long and dreadful process, the conjuration began on a very, very bad day.

Carlton had been murdered. Bertrand staggered down the steps to their apothecary in a wild state of panic. He carried Carlton's limp body in his arms, his brother's head almost completely severed at the neck. Blood was everywhere.

Bertrand had yelled and moaned, he'd begged Estela for her help. Elias recalled her cautioning him, her careful and reassuring tones morphing into insistence and finally into desperate pleading. But Bertrand would not listen. He demanded his brother be resurrected. He demanded she start immediately.

And so she had. She had no choice. She could not betray the bond.

Estela's morbid sorcery had taken weeks to accomplish. The body, even covered in poultices and bandages, began to putrefy after just a few days. After a week it was nauseating even to be in the corridor outside. But Elias' mother never left the corpse. She sat in vigil, focused on what would be the most complicated series of incantations of her life. Elias brought her food, drink, and any components she required, and tried not to vomit whenever he approached the bloated sack of flesh that had once been Carlton.

There had been an uprising in the Southern Plains. Without

Chapter Fifteen

Carlton's tyranny, and with Estela's power diverted to his resurrection, the resistance in the fiefdom was strengthening.

The only thing worse than Carlton's bloated and seeping remains was Carlton's resurrected flesh. No less putrid, the monster finally awoke one day. Elias' mother collapsed from exhaustion as the beast arose and looked vacuously at the stone walls surrounding them.

The monster did not live for long. None of them did. As soon as she had the strength to move, Estela ordered the reanimated corpse to the main castle where Bertrand waited. Not five minutes after their macabre reunion, the main gate was breached and ragged townspeople stormed inside to butcher everyone within and avenge their dead. Drained almost completely of her power, Estela put up no fight at all.

The last Elias saw of her, she and her monster were being smothered and destroyed by the ravaging mass. Elias raced frantically back down the stairs, pushed through the Big Door, hustled down to the crypt, and picked his way across the pile of tortured remains before slipping between the rusted bars of an ancient iron drainage grate to a secret escape into the forest beyond.

*What lay before him would be days and days without food or drink,
without the comforts of civilization or the company of friends.*

Chapter Sixteen
OHLEN

The experience with Magda had linked Ohlen to a force he had not known before. He became keenly aware of the will of the natural world: the plants, the animals, the trees, and even the springs and streams that fed them. In communing with Magda he had encountered a beauty and simplicity untouchable by sentient beings—an elegance in life made dim by the ambition of humankind.

The forest and its creatures, the grasses and the rivers, they indeed possessed an ancient and powerful collective will. It was a will to allow lives to run their natural course in their natural time. It was a will to recycle nature's gifts, to build new life from old, to fashion the dust of the deceased into the lifeblood of youth, to see the rigidity and wisdom of age protect and guide the hopes and dreams of the young.

And it was good.

Chapter Sixteen

The ancient presence could be an ally in their fight against whatever accursed evil was befalling them—Magda had made that clear. So as painful and frightening as the decision was to abandon his friends on the road to Rockmoor, there was no question in Ohlen's mind it was the correct path. The task before him as he strode away, was to seek solitude, and meditate on this newly discovered mythic presence.

So he had walked.

Ohlen had spent the better part of the day walking south from the road through rolling fields of tall grass dotted here and there with rocky protrusions scattered about like tiny reminders of the rugged mountains to the west.

At sundown he had slowed his pace, and veered east toward the lush forest that stretched between the plains and the sea. His feet carried him to the place that would be his home for the next days or weeks. One final rocky finger protruded from the wavy sea of green grass, right at the edge of the forest.

I have been brought, Ohlen realized, *to the perfect convergence of rock, field and forest.*

With some effort, Ohlen hoisted himself onto the enormous craggy rock. Several birds hastily took flight as his fingers slid in layers of muck left behind by their long-undisturbed residency. But Ohlen was not bothered in the least. What lay before him would be days and days without food or drink, without the comforts of civilization or the company of friends. Ohlen was no stranger to mental and physical deprivation. Indeed, he found the regular routine of the body's natural cycles to be an imposition on the development of the spirit.

He was, however, keenly interested in finding a comfortable place to sit. He recalled from his many lengthy meditations that sitting on uneven or jagged surfaces could cause great distraction during meditation and significant discomfort afterward. So he stood and paced carefully about the small ledge and eventually settled on just the spot where, by layering some articles from his bag on the rock, he prepared a seat his bottom could agree with.

His mind traveled first to his companions. His generous, heroic, resolute companions. Among them, Ruprecht loomed large. The man he had been, and the shadow of himself he had become after his corruption. Ohlen gently eased his fixation, borne of fear and worry, from his troubled friend, and brought to himself, instead, the warmth from the shining qualities embodied in Gnome, X'andria, Arden, and Boudreaux.

He was not sure if he became aware of the ancient presence, or if it became aware of him, but by morning, his consciousness began moving away from the people in his life, and pushed ever so slowly instead into the deep natural stone beneath him. This was a new awareness, a sensation like none other. Had he not experienced the force of nature's spirit focused through Magda, he would never have been able to recognize the simple and gentle pulse of stone reaching up from the earth beneath him.

The spiritual communion extended over two days.

Two full days of unceasing concentration passed before he felt not only what he thought to be the complete presence of the stone beneath him, but also the earth beyond. As the soil was less dense than the rock, his consciousness pushed outward ever so slightly faster. And here he encountered hunger and satiety, fear and safety. Here, in the small animals and in the bugs and worms, were lives free from the complexity of ego, yet still wrought with the primal urges of survival and self-preservation.

Then the forest greeted him. *These are like the spirits I*

encountered at Magda's, he recognized. Five glorious days passed in which Ohlen embedded his consciousness in the vast and ancient rhythm of the natural world. The birds returned and alighted on the massive rock, and on his body, depositing waste on both that would be rinsed by the rains, and become nourishment for new growth. With time Ohlen gave over his singularity to the vast collective.

Until the biting fingers of pain penetrated deeply enough to wrench him back to the surface of consciousness.

Sound and smell were the first to awaken. There were dull thuds of fleshy impact on stone. There were bloody squelches. There was the putrid odor of rotten death.

As Ohlen's eyes slowly began to flutter and illuminate, he realized the pain was coming from his right leg, which was wet and screaming from being violently gouged.

Shock and pain are a potent combination to rouse someone from even the deepest cogitation. With the stiffness in his limbs, and the heavy fog in his mind rebelling mightily, Ohlen willed himself to alertness and looked down at the cause of his pain.

Dead eyes. Even though the dirty nails of its thick fingers pulled free a bloody chunk of Ohlen's leg, it was the total absence of life in the blank white eyes that arrested Ohlen's attention. He struggled desperately, forcing his body to obey as he grabbed the wrist of the monster and tried to wrestle it free of his leg, without separating any more of his flesh than was already stripped.

Inhumanly strong. The cold grip was like iron. *It wants me,* Ohlen realized. He managed to wrest away the fingers from burrowing into his thigh, but as soon as he grasped the hand, it tried to pull him down from the rock completely. Woozy from his meditation, Ohlen nearly fell, but somehow managed to extricate his fingers from the vise-like grip and still keep his perch.

Ohlen was standing painfully now. The monster was relentless. Now it tried to climb onto the rock with him. It placed bloody fingers on the ledge and began to hoist itself up. Ohlen stamped hard on the fingers with his left foot, nearly toppling on his wounded right side. Any normal creature in the world would have pulled its hand back off the ledge from the pain, but not this one. It registered nothing at all, and instead just kept coming. As Ohlen retracted his boot from the fingers, so, too, came squashed dead flesh that had been covering the bones and tendons.

This being is already dead! It did not breathe, it made no sound. It did not yell in pain, gasp in frustration, or grunt with effort. It just kept coming. Ohlen's sword was leaning against the rock behind him. More alert now, he grasped the hilt, removed it from its scabbard, and swung the blade swiftly down into the forearm connected to the now-skeletal hand.

The beast fell to the earth, but immediately stood and approached the rock again. Now ending in a bloodless stump, its right arm lodged over a lower hold in the craggy stone, and its feet scrabbled for purchase beneath. Ohlen retreated to the far side of the ledge.

Moments later, the monster's ghostly, decaying left hand swung with a thud onto the top of the ledge, it grasped Ohlen's bag, and then both disappeared out of sight.

Strapping his sword to his waist, Ohlen crept to the near edge of his perch and peered over the side. He was now becoming aware of his weakness, of how starved his body was of nutrients, of how his right leg was teetering on the edge of debilitation.

On the ground ten feet beneath him, the frightful fiend had pinned Ohlen's leather bag to the earth with its stump and was savagely stripping pieces of it away with its left hand and with its

Chapter Sixteen

teeth, like a dog ripping sinew from a bone.

Then, in abject horror, Ohlen realized what it was after. *My ivory case!* The beast, an animated corpse, was standing now. Having uncovered its prize, it turned and began shambling back toward the forest.

Ohlen flew madly through the air. His arms contacted the cold mountain of flesh, before his legs hit the ground, his right giving out completely. Lying prone in the grass, he saw the beast turn slightly to regard him with its dead eyes, and then proceed onward toward the trees, the ivory case clutched tightly in its remaining hand.

With effort, Ohlen's sword passed halfway to the hilt into its wide back right where the heart should be. There was very little effect. The beast just turned around once more as though it had heard something curious behind it. Ohlen managed to keep hold of his sword as it spun, and, after regaining his footing, extracted the blade, now smeared black with thick, dead blood.

It had entered the forest. It was lumbering faster, and dropped into a crouch to use its stump as a third leg to navigate the terrain.

Ohlen would not be able to catch it. His right leg nearly useless, weak from starvation, and bleeding liberally as he was, this was not a flight he would be able to pursue for long.

With his last burst of energy, Ohlen caught up once more to the horror, and hacked with all his might at its left arm just above the elbow. Its momentum carried it a few feet further, but the arm, Ohlen's ivory case, and the horrid black orbs within, stayed behind on the forest floor.

Ohlen fell on the pale severed arm and scrambled backward on his behind to put distance between himself and the now handless monster before him.

But it turned and clambered its way to Ohlen with surprising speed. Ohlen kicked feebly as it pummeled him with its sticky stumps. It was using its weight now to pin him down, trying to bite any part of him it could reach.

But without hands, the creature could not contain him. Holding tight to the severed arm, Ohlen rolled awkwardly away and began to stagger deeper into the woods.

The beast pursued him, but fell to the ground. Turning, Ohlen saw that its foot had been snagged by a large tree root. *That root was not there a moment ago!* On they went. The monster's progress continued to be impeded by obstacles appearing before it on the forest floor. So while his own pace was painfully slow, the deathly horror slowly faded in the distance behind him as Ohlen stumbled his way toward the coast.

Hastening through the deserted, moonlit expanse, past the lodge, and into Westwood, Arden checked nervously over his shoulder as he went. He could not shake the feeling that something was pursuing him.

Chapter Seventeen
THE PLOT THICKENS

On several occasions, Arden had joined Boudreaux for ales after training. They had gone together to a basement tavern called The Iron Axe not far from their cottage. The stuffy smell of sweat-soaked wooden tables and chairs on an old floor that had seen much worse, caused Arden to yearn for the fresh air of the outdoors. But Boudreaux seemed oblivious to the odor and went there happily night after night.

Neither of them had ever seen square, wooden cups before. Made of simple panels held together by thin black iron fittings, Boudreaux was crazy about them, and was thoroughly convinced they imparted a special flavor to the ale served within. Arden concurred that the cups imparted a flavor, but he was not so sure it was a flavor he cared ever to taste again.

This night, Arden's startling discovery in the woods had left his nerves frayed with anxiety. Already exhausted from a long day of intense exercise, he emerged from the forest into the darkened training field breathless and sweaty.

Hastening through the deserted, moonlit expanse, past the lodge, and into Westwood, Arden checked nervously over his shoulder as he went. He could not shake the feeling that something was pursuing him.

It was only as he descended the worn wooden steps to The Iron Axe's heavy oak door that Arden's pulse and breath began to return to normal. He pushed inside, relieved to be entering a space with other people around, and scanned the room for his companion.

Boudreaux was a creature of habit. He was sitting at his usual table, talking animatedly to the older of two daughters who served ale, stew, and bread each night to the woodsmen, hunters, and carpenters who frequented the dingy tavern. The young woman, who looked like she wanted to be anywhere but here, smiled feebly at the jovial, babbling Boudreaux, and took her first opportunity to escape back to the kitchen.

"There's Arden!" Boudreaux boomed, as his friend threaded his way between the crush of tables, chairs, and hunched bodies—the Iron Axe was crowded tonight. Perhaps it was just his paranoia, but everywhere Arden looked he saw unfriendly faces, dangerous eyes, baleful glares. With Boudreaux's announcement, the low hum of conversation stopped briefly as the motley assemblage regarded the new arrival.

"Boudreaux, I need to talk to you," Arden murmured as he bent to take a seat.

"Arden, I think you need a drink," his friend beamed back at him, and raised his enormous arm to flag down one of the sisters. "Ale!" he shouted.

Two hooded figures sat nearby, and although Arden could not see their shadowed faces, he could tell by the incline of their heads that they were both listening.

"I think we need to go, Boudreaux." Arden persisted, "I need to speak with you in private."

"The older one is crazy about me, Arden." Boudreaux was obviously drunk. "Did you see how she was looking at me?"

Arden reached across the table and gripped Boudreaux's forearm just as his friend was lifting his square cup of ale to his lips for another swig.

"*Now*, Boudreaux, we have to go now."

The change was remarkable, really. Boudreaux seemed to will himself to sobriety. Recognizing the urgency in Arden's face for the first time, he placed the wooden vessel deliberately back on the table. Rummaging wordlessly in his trousers for a few coppers before casually spilling them onto the table, Boudreaux stood and headed straight for the door as if leaving had been his idea to begin with.

They entered their cottage to find Gnome and X'andria deep in conversation. Words were hurriedly spilling from X'andria when they banged through the door, and even though she abruptly stopped talking at their appearance, it was clear from the look on her face that she was upset.

"What's up, X'andria?" Arden asked.

X'andria was silent, shaken, and looked through red puffy eyes from Gnome sitting beside her to the two large men looming in the entry way.

"X'andria's just had a rough day, guys," Gnome said simply. "What's up with you two, how was training?"

"What happened? Did magic man finally make some magic moves?" Boudreaux joked sardonically, unable to control himself.

"Tonight isn't the night, Boudreaux," Gnome warned in a low voice, as X'andria slumped and looked away at the far wall.

"I'm sorry to hear it, X'andria." Arden was clearly concerned. "Believe it or not, I've had a troubling day, too." Arden and Boudreaux both sat down noisily on the floor near the others. "I was just telling Boudreaux about it on the way home."

It was after midnight, and everyone slept except for Gnome. Before bed, Arden had described the unnatural presence in the forest to all of them. X'andria, having told Gnome privately about her terror on the docks, remained silent in front of the other two. Boudreaux voiced his concerns again about Ruprecht's long absences and bizarre behavior. They all rallied around the hope that Ohlen would catch up with them soon.

Gnome's soft leather garments allowed him to rise without a sound. He wore deep-sea eel-skin slippers that had been a gift from The Master. They molded to his feet in such a way as to allow his soles to roll catlike along the earth almost as though he wore nothing over them at all.

The Master had chosen to train Gnome to scale walls. Naturally gifted at moving without detection, this was a new skill Gnome was particularly eager to learn. The slippers were indispensible, since difficult climbing involved exploiting the smallest of toe-holds. The eel skin was tacky, and helped him cling to almost any dry surface as long as he oiled it regularly. The slippers also distributed his weight beyond whatever minute piece of flesh or nail he was able to wedge into the faint cracks and divots his probing toes encountered when he climbed.

Gnome sped, like a piece of the night itself, through the now-familiar alleys and underpasses that led him east from Westwood into the heart of The Grotto and toward the thieves' den. Racing, climbing, and swinging along, he was deep in thought. The stories he'd heard were swirling around like puzzle pieces in his mind.

Poor X'andria! What a cruel twist of fate that the very same men who tore her from her mother's arms as a child and forced her into slavery would appear before her on the docks of Rockmoor. And Arden got so worked up describing the destruction he found in the forest. *He'll go back and investigate that tomorrow, thought Gnome. Tonight I'll see what the thieves know about docks and tattoos.*

And that was the last thought to go through his mind before his feet locked up and his face bit hard into the packed dirt road of The Grotto.

"Well look who's sneakin' 'round here, boys?" The voice was loud enough to be jeering, and soft enough not to wake the neighborhood.

It was Rove, the rude, skinny thief Gnome had met on his first visit to The Den. Rove had tossed a weighted trip cord at just the right time to bind both of Gnome's feet tightly together at the ankles.

"What the hell, Rove?" Gnome ground out through gritted teeth, as he spat bloody dirt out of his mouth.

"Yer not gonna like it, freak, so we'll let it be a surprise." The skinny man hovered a few feet away in partial shadow, moonlight reflecting the danger in his narrowed eyes.

"You're violating The Code, Rove, Master won't be pleased," Gnome burbled through his spittle into the dirt.

"Master won't be pleased," Rove mocked in an over-enunciated sing-song impersonation of his captive to the snickering delight of his little band of followers. "Master won't never know, freak, once The Torrent has its way with ya." Rove's words were laced with menace. More anxiously, he snapped, "C'mon Fig, do 'is hands!"

Fig, a witless boy who had come under Rove's influence, fumbled forward with a second weighted trip cord. Gnome had seen Fig a few times skulking around The Den, but had never heard him speak.

Gnome secretively inched his hand toward the hilt of his dagger, which was pinned between his left hip and the ground. His feet were hopelessly locked together. This was a dangerous disadvantage. He did not want to hurt Fig, but as the boy approached, he knew it could not be helped.

Fig bent awkwardly to loop the cord around Gnome's wrists. Rolling his body swiftly, Gnome extracted and sliced his dagger savagely through the night. The blade cleanly severed the boy's left pinky and ring fingers, and half of the middle finger. The shocked adolescent dropped the cord and jumped backward, howling and cradling his maimed hand, blood spurting between his fingers.

"You idiot, Fig, shut up!" Rove hissed dispassionately at the whimpering boy. "You'll wake the whole Grotto!" Gnome was attempting to wriggle away on the ground now, all the while shimmying his legs back and forth in an effort to loosen the thin cord binding them.

But Rove advanced predatorily toward Gnome and growled, "Alright, ya pointy-eared freak, have it your way," as he kicked him, hard, on the left side of his head.

The night swam. Gnome's ears rang like he was inside a giant bell. Hurting and disoriented as he was, though, somehow Gnome understood that Rove was ordering his small band of thugs to drag him by his feet to the Torrent River.

Rough hands grabbed his ankles. They flipped him over, and began pulling him, face down, over the foul earth. They had not dragged him very far when Gnome heard a thud, a shout, then felt them drop his feet.

Gnome warily propped himself up. To his surprise, he saw that Rove was lying on the ground next to him, blood dripping down his face from a nasty forehead wound.

Some unseen assailant had rendered Rove unconscious. Gnome was able to hold himself up long enough to see the sorry band scatter into the night, Fig weaving deliriously at the rear.

Moments later, Gnome felt hurried and shaking hands working to unwind the weighted trip cord from around his ankles.

"Can you move, Mister Gnome?" Waif's face appeared just inches from his own.

Some minutes passed before Waif was able to assist Gnome down an alley to a sheltered alcove where he could rest and gather his wits. They left Rove behind at the scene of the ambush.

"Thank you, Waif, I think you just saved my life," Gnome finally managed, once it felt like his head would not explode.

Waif just hovered silently.

"How did you do it? How did you know?" Gnome asked.

Waif produced a leather sling and mimicked swinging it in the air. Flashing a smile, he said sheepishly, "I heard them talking, Mister

Gnome, they wanted to hurt you."

"Well, they managed that, didn't they?" Gnome said bitterly, "but not near as bad as I think they wanted to."

"Rove hates you, Mister Gnome, and I think he don't like how much time The Master is with you."

They sat silently for a few minutes as Gnome stabilized.

"I need your help, Waif," he finally said. "Do you ever spend any time down by the docks?"

X'andria was relieved to discover Gnome was gone when she rose late that night. It was simple enough to sneak out past Arden, even though he was a light sleeper, and Boudreaux was capable of snoring through anything. But Gnome, especially since their arrival in Rockmoor, seemed to notice even the smallest of sounds and motions around him, and X'andria knew that Gnome would not approve of what she was about to do.

Carefully pulling the door closed behind her, she stepped out into the still night. Gliding along the boardwalk, she nervously fingered her small golden loop, turning it over and over like a tiny set of prayer beads.

X'andria raised the hood of her cloak to conceal her face. Approaching the north edge of Westwood, she swallowed hard and turned her feet back toward the docks.

So he walked on in silence back toward their cottage until the sight of two cloaked figures coming toward him gave him pause.

Chapter Eighteen
UNEXPECTED ENCOUNTERS

———————————

It was a rare morning when Boudreaux woke up before Arden. With less ale than usual to sleep off, and with his nerves still bristling from Arden's troubling tale, he found himself with his eyes open, staring up at the ceiling in the hazy silence of first light.

The truth was, however, that he awoke thinking about X'andria. More than anyone else he knew, hers was a spirit of sunny enthusiasm and unbridled curiosity. To see fear cast dark shadows over her usually bright eyes was deeply troubling.

And where's that damn Ruprecht? Boudreaux thought irritably. They knew he was hanging out at some temple in Hillcrest. But he was gone for days on end, and he seemed to Boudreaux to be turning more suspicious and secretive on each of the rare occasions they saw each other. *Next time I see him, we'll have a serious talk,* Boudreaux thought. *It's time for Ruprecht to snap out of it and start helping the friends who saved his life.*

He propped himself up on his elbows and looked around the room. Gnome was gone. That was typical. In fact Boudreaux could not think of a single day when he had risen, that Gnome was still at home. Ruprecht's bed was also empty. *Of course it is,* Boudreaux frowned. *He's still with that Hillcrest creep he thinks so highly of.*

X'andria was gone.

What the hell? Boudreaux ejected himself into the air and onto his feet like he was some kind of acrobat. Pounding across the room and patting the furs of her bed, his hands confirmed what his eyes knew to be true.

Concern welled up quickly inside Boudreaux. It filled his broad chest and head with an anxious desire to act, to hit something, to destroy it. He turned around several times as if he might somehow come upon the culprit responsible for her absence.

"Hey, Arden." He settled for waking up his friend. "Arden, get up, man. X'andria's gone."

"Wh-wha's up?" Arden flailed beneath his furs and lurched to his feet. Arden's nerves were wired like a wild animal's, and even though he was still half-dreaming, he stood, stark naked, with his fists clenched like he was ready for whatever threat might be approaching.

Immediately Boudreaux regretted waking his friend. First, he hated to be woken up himself. Second, he was now staring at a completely nude Arden.

"Sorry, man," Boudreaux turned his eyes to the floor. "I'm sorry I woke you up. It's just... X'andria's gone."

Arden's head was slowly beginning to clear.

"That's weird," he replied, reaching casually for his trousers. "She's usually not even awake yet when we leave for The Fields." Reading Boudreaux's alarmed expression Arden continued, "If there's one thing I've learned about X'andria, it's that she always keeps you guessing. I'm sure she'll be back over there reading by the time we come home tonight."

It was a tough training day for Arden. Boudreaux was relentless. The force of his blows seemed somehow to have magnified. And that was saying something. The powerful half-elf was stoically silent for most of the day and appeared focused on causing devastation with every strike.

"I think I might be nearing the end, Boudreaux," Arden winced. It was mid-afternoon, he had at least two cracked ribs that whined when he moved, and he did not even want to see the bruising that was surely waiting for him beneath his armor.

Boudreaux relaxed his stance and dropped the tip of his blade heavily into the earth where, by its weight alone, it lodged several inches deep. He stared inscrutably out into the trees and seemed not even to be breathing heavily.

"She'll be alright, Boudreaux. X'andria can take care of herself." Arden's soft words floated to him like a light breeze against a stone wall.

Boudreaux remained motionless. Arden stood squinting, and hurting, unsure if his friend had even heard him.

"I guess I just don't know," Boudreaux finally spoke, "if any of us will be alright, Arden." He shifted his gaze to meet Arden's eyes now.

Chapter Eighteen

"I've never told anyone about it, but when we were in that hole, at the end, I came face to face with that stone fiend."

Arden watched in silence as the color drained from his friend's face.

"It owned me completely, Arden, like I was some feeble doll. I was thrust back into moments of my childhood I'd tried to forget long ago. I was forced to relive some of my worst memories. And it made me fight myself, Arden. Terrifying. But it was not really me, exactly, it was that thing pretending to be me. It was toying with me, playing with me in some kind of arena where it was not only my opponent, but it was the arena too, and the audience, and the earth, and the sky." Boudreaux ran out of words.

"But you survived, Boudreaux. We all did." Arden looked imploringly into the depths of his friend's eyes. "And we will survive again. Ohlen told us all to get stronger, and that's what we've been doing. Goodness knows, I better be stronger after all the abuse you've been doling out today." He allowed himself a grin.

They walked back to the lodge in silence. Arden was limping slightly, but he could tell that Boudreaux's mood was at least a little lighter than when the day had begun.

In spite of his pain and fatigue, Arden went back into the forest that night. Retracing his steps from the evening before was easy. Even though he was always careful to tread lightly, day-old human bootprints were simple to discern indeed.

But tonight Arden was on high alert. Not yet close to the scene of the destruction, he took note of the animals rustling in the bushes, the chorus of the crickets, the hooting of the owls. The further he walked, and the more attention he paid, the more he realized how oddly silent the wood was becoming.

It must be near.

Arden froze, nostrils flaring. He closed his eyes to focus his attention on sound and smell. The forest was so eerily quiet.

He picked up a foreign scent. Faint. Days old. But as he locked onto it, he recognized the unmistakably rich and pungent odor of putrefaction.

Arden nearly gagged.

What in the world have I found? he wondered, as he dropped gingerly to his hands and knees and continued forward, crawling on all fours like a bloodhound.

He was moving in the right direction. The olfactory stamp was not so much getting stronger as it was becoming more broadly present. It felt as though the forest itself was intentionally issuing forth the evidence to lead him in his investigation.

Arden's ribs complained bitterly. He would not be able to continue to crawl with his face near the earth. But just as he was about to stand up, he heard something coming.

It was crashing. Limbs were breaking and leaves were crackling. It rushed toward him with an oddly lurching gait.

Sweat moistened the back of Arden's neck. *Here we go then,* he thought grimly, as he jumped up into fighting stance, steel flashing quickly into both of his powerful hands. Whatever it was, Arden had decided he did not like it very much.

The thing was approaching. He heard it breathing hard, with heavy, rasping heaves. It seemed almost to be stumbling. Close by now, the trajectory would take it by him to his left.

Arden maneuvered to engage. Ignoring the pain in his chest, he bounded toward the interloper, bracing himself for whatever monstrosity he might find.

But Arden did not encounter some huge lumbering beast or freak of nature. Instead he intercepted a phenomenally dirty, skinny man with short white hair. He wore tattered clothing, and was clutching a grotesque severed arm.

Between the rotten limb and abundant general filth, the man smelled horrendous. He stumbled along with one of his legs maimed and barely useable, blood stained his dirty white robes.

With one sword still held aloft as a precaution, Arden shouted at the unfortunate soul to stop.

The man tried to freeze, but instead teetered dangerously on legs unwilling to hold him much longer. He turned his dirty face to Arden, revealing a crazed and terrified expression. Arden stared back in shocked disbelief.

"Ohlen?" He fumbled for words. "My god, what's happened to you?"

The Iron Axe was not too crowded tonight. Only Gertrude, the younger of the two sisters, was working. Gertrude was not very pleasant, Boudreaux had decided, but that did not stop him from ordering what was, even for him, an impressive amount of ale.

With each cup of the dark golden brew, the pointy edges of worry about their current predicament became duller. As he drank, Boudreaux convinced himself that X'andria would be back at the cottage when he got home that night. He entertained the fantasy that Ohlen would return soon as well. And he even imagined some stern and satisfying conversations between himself and Ruprecht that involved some good old-fashioned two-fisted convincing.

Boudreaux smiled at the thought.

Leaving the Iron Axe, he took a slightly longer route home. With the amount of ale he had ingested, a walk before bed would do him some good. He ventured north almost to Hillcrest before finding a dark corner to relieve himself in. Feeling much lighter, he turned around and began swaying back along the boardwalks of Westwood.

There were not too many people out this late, and none he passed showed any interest in conversation. So he walked on in silence back toward their cottage until the sight of two cloaked figures coming toward him gave him pause.

Boudreaux stopped and stared drunkenly at them as they approached. And then it dawned on him.

"Ruprecht?" he called. "Is that you?"

The two stopped in mid-step.

Boudreaux advanced jauntily toward them. "Is that you, Ruprecht?" he asked again. "Lower your hoods."

Boudreaux was almost upon them when one of them finally answered proudly, "Yes, Boudreaux, it is I, Ruprecht." And Ruprecht lowered his hood with a distrustful scowl.

"Well why don't you introduce me to your friend that I've heard so much about?" Boudreaux was talking too loudly. The scowl annoyed him. Ruprecht annoyed him. And the ale was not helping anything.

"Calm down, Boudreaux. This is Dortmund. Dortmund is the cleric of the Hillcrest Temple, Boudreaux. I don't expect you to understand, but he's a very important person, and we were just on our way back to the temple." Ruprecht spoke as though Boudreaux were a dim-witted child.

Chapter Eighteen

They stood there awkwardly, Boudreaux making no move to allow them easy passage.

"Does Mister Important speak?" Boudreaux mocked. "Do you speak, Dorton?"

"Dort-mund," came the deliberate hiss from beneath the hood. "My name is Dortmund. And we have things to attend to, sir, if you will excuse us."

"Soon enough," Boudreaux slurred. "But I have some things to tell Ruprecht first."

"We're going," Dortmund commanded, and grabbed Ruprecht's arm.

"Wait, wait, wait," Boudreaux persisted, reaching out now to block their progress.

Dortmund extended one pale skinny hand and lightly touched Boudreaux's outstretched arm. What Boudreaux felt next was agony. Long, pulsating jolts of searing pain originated in his arm and scoured every inch of his body before exiting him through his feet into the wooden boards beneath them. Fully conscious during this torture, Boudreaux was aware of his huge frame involuntarily convulsing up and down, even though he was completely powerless to move or even to talk.

When Dortmund finally released him from the torment, the huge man crumpled to the ground like a heavy sail that has been released from its mast. He lay motionless, gasping like a fish pulled from the ocean, his eyes staring straight ahead.

The last Boudreaux remembered of the encounter was Ruprecht's terrified and bewildered expression as he lingered above Boudreaux's inert body, before scampering away to follow the hooded Dortmund into the darkness.

Mind whirring, Gnome decided to risk lighting a candle,
and contented himself to wait for at least a little while.

Chapter Nineteen
PIECES

———————————

After leaving Waif, Gnome had traced his steps back to the site of the ambush but the bastard Rove was nowhere to be found. Unwilling to risk being followed—and hopeful he might learn something useful—Gnome hid in the shadow of a nearby alleyway for a full day before threading his way home. Though quite hungry, Gnome's wits were recovered from the startling attack of the previous night.

When he finally crept back into the cottage, he was surprised to find no one home. This was very unusual. In the dead of night, when he often returned, he could always count on Boudreaux and Arden being fast asleep in their beds. Seeing and hearing the big snoring benevolent mounds made him smile. X'andria was usually in at this time of night, too, though frequently she would still be up, studying by the light of a solitary candle that caused her face to glow dimly across the room, her sharp features cut with the dancing shadows of the flickering flame.

But tonight the cottage was dark and deserted. Gnome's anxiety billowed within him, and immediately he suspected Rove and his dastardly machinations. *Does he know where I live? Had he followed me home in the past?* Gnome could not imagine a scenario where Rove, with any number of his sorry brethren, could have possibly bested X'andria, Boudreaux, and Arden. Plus there were no signs of struggle. *But perhaps if they were ambushed one at a time, like I was...*

Mind whirring, Gnome decided to risk lighting a candle, and contented himself to wait for at least a little while.

He did not have to wait long.

Boudreaux crashed in several minutes later. "Gettup Arden," he shouted as the heavy oak door whined on its hinges. "Arden, that bastard Dorton..." Boudreaux stopped short, the door still open and swinging behind him.

"Where's Arden?" He addressed Gnome with an unusual sharpness.

"Arden's not here, Boudreaux." Gnome retorted. "Are you drunk?"

"Well I was," Boudreaux was raging, "until Ruprecht and his friend attacked me in the street. I've been lying in my own drool for the last hour. I'm gonna tear those two apart and stick the wrong halves back together if they like each other so much." Coming to his senses, he asked sincerely, "Where is everybody, Gnome? Where the hell is X'andria?"

"I've no idea." Gnome seemed genuinely confused. "I don't know what's going on. I got ambushed late last night, Boudreaux, by a gang of damn thieves."

"What?" Boudreaux sat down and only then became aware of

Gnome's swollen and bloody face.

"I just came home, and now everyone's gone except you. And you're telling me Ruprecht and that idiot from the temple attacked you. How the hell did they get the better of you, Boudreaux?"

"Good question," Boudreaux harrumphed. "I just wasn't expecting it, and I guess I was pretty drunk, too," he admitted. "I was just trying to tell Ruprecht to stop being a jerk, that his friends need him, that X'andria's gone and Arden's freaked out, and that it's time for him to get his act together. At least that's what I wanted to tell him. But I didn't get any of that out, because that guy Dortmund did something to me. I couldn't do anything, Gnome! He grabbed my arm and sent these waves of pain all through me. It felt like my body was getting stabbed over and over again and like I was being baked in an oven at the same time. I just flopped on the ground and couldn't move until a few minutes ago." Boudreaux did not seem seriously harmed, but he was clearly shocked and a little embarrassed.

Gnome was a good listener. He looked up through swollen and crusty eyes with sincere concern at his enormous friend.

"That sounds terrible, Boudreaux. I'm sorry to hear it," he finally replied. "And so disappointing that Ruprecht could have watched it happen, and would even be associating with someone so... unscrupulous."

They sat in silence for a few moments, before Boudreaux continued: "Ruprecht looked scared, actually. I was on the ground, and he looked almost like he wanted to stop and help me. But Dortmund insisted they run away, and Ruprecht took off with him." Stopping for breath, Boudreaux eyed Gnome through the gloom. "What happened to you?"

"Oh," Gnome stifled a derisive laugh, "there's this imbecile named Rove in the Den. I didn't like him the day we met, and he certainly didn't like me. But I guess I didn't realize how much until last night. He got together a band of cowards and they ambushed me. Tripped me up as I was heading to The Den. They bound my ankles and beat me up a bit, and told me they were going to dump me in The Torrent to drown."

"Whoa," Boudreaux exhaled with a whistle, "That's worse than what happened to me. How'd you get away?"

"Well I got lucky is the truth of it," Gnome responded thoughtfully. "Waif is this young and talented thief. He's actually the one I followed our second day here in Rockmoor when I first found The Den. We've become friends, I guess, and he had overheard them plotting to take me down. He felled Rove with a lucky shot from his sling to the creep's forehead, and the rest of the cowards fled. I just had no idea they would do something so crazy."

More silence passed.

"Gnome," Boudreaux finally broke in, "what's going on with X'andria?"

But Gnome was gone. Boudreaux blinked twice to assure himself his eyes were not deceiving him. Some part of his mind even entertained the notion that the entire conversation had been imaginary, some trick his brain was playing on him between the ale and Dortmund's attack.

But then he detected Gnome, halfway up the wall to his left, in the darkest part of the room. Gnome had melted away in a flash.

And now Boudreaux heard it too. Someone was approaching. The big man was on his feet in an instant, and crept behind the door. When he wanted to, he could be surprisingly silent. He swiftly unsheathed the silver sword from Bridgeton he kept strapped to his back—the shorter blade would be easier to wield in the cramped space of their cottage.

A moment later the door flew open. "Guys," came the shout, "it's Ohlen! He's hurt bad!" Arden piled through the door half-carrying and half-dragging a nearly unconscious Ohlen with him.

Gnome dropped like an insect from the ceiling and immediately began clearing their heavy wooden table.

Gnome lit more candles. They covered the table with furs, and Boudreaux gently laid Ohlen's thin body on top. Arden cleaned and dressed Ohlen's many wounds, spending a long time on the gaping divot in his right leg.

The half-conscious Ohlen seemed totally set upon gripping the disgusting, smelly, rotten forearm that was, itself, holding onto his precious ivory case. Realizing this, Gnome whispered into Ohlen's ears for almost half an hour to explain that he was safe now, that he was back among friends, that everything was going to be alright, that they would extract the case, and discard the arm.

The message must have gotten through, because eventually Ohlen relaxed his tight grasp on the putrid arm. Gnome covered it quickly in one of X'andria's blank parchment rolls. After very carefully extracting the ivory case, Gnome gave the arm to Boudreaux to carry outside and dispose of.

At dawn Ohlen opened his eyes. Oddly they were crystal clear, bright even, and did not match the torn and beleaguered body they belonged to. Immediately Gnome offered him water, which he was able to sip slowly through parched and cracked lips.

It was mid-morning before he spoke.

"Where is X'andria?" were his first words.

Chapter Nineteen

Boudreaux and Arden turned to Gnome. Gnome swallowed, and seemed to come to a hard internal decision. "I'm not sure she would want you all to know," Gnome replied carefully, "but given the circumstances, I think I have to explain."

Gnome then shared what he knew about X'andria's past from the story she had told him that bright day in Bridgeton. He told them of her childhood in Atolia, of her abduction on the beach, and of her enslavement as a child before the two of them met and came under the tutelage of The Alchemist. Apparently, Gnome continued, she had been down by the docks receiving instruction on how to conjure fire when she spotted a huge tattooed sailor, an Islander, coming toward her down the pier. She did not recognize him in particular, but she did recognize the tattoos: the very same kind she'd seen on those sailors who snatched her from her mother's arms so many years ago.

"That's just terrible," Arden was the first to break the long silence that followed Gnome's tale. "I had no idea."

"What about you, Ohlen?" Boudreaux cut in. "You look like you've been through hell."

"I am stronger than I look," Ohlen smiled weakly, and his bright eyes twinkled. "I have had quite a physical trial in the past few days, it is true, but that came after a deep communion. Thanks to your care and kindness, and especially to Arden finding me in the woods, I imagine it will not be too long before my outside more accurately reflects my inside."

Boudreaux did not pretend to understand anything Ohlen had just said. "Alright," he pressed on, "but what the hell happened?"

So Ohlen, between pauses for breath, and to moisten his lips, explained his journey. He began with Magda, with his belief that nature would be an important ally, with the necessity of his solitary meditation. He explained, in spite of their increasingly strained and confused expressions, about the spiritual connections he had made with stone, and field, and forest. As he spoke, miraculously, it appeared as though his body was regaining its strength.

"And then I was attacked by a huge, dead, rotting corpse," he said simply. "It was probably a week into my meditation when he came upon me. The only reason I'm alive is that I had chosen to take up residence atop a high sheer rock. So I became aware of him clawing at my leg before he had an opportunity to tear me apart completely." He stopped, seemingly lost in thought.

"And then?" prompted Arden, who was now busying himself over a low flame to make them all a breakfast of rye gruel with dried berries that he had collected during his trips into the forest.

"Well, I do not understand it," he sighed. "I have never come face to face with something that was already dead before. But I know several things. It was after the orbs," he patted the ivory case beside him, "and it must have been animated by some powerful dark necromancer. It very nearly killed me, but I somehow got away, and believe it or not, I think the forest actually helped me. Incredible, really." Ohlen's eyes misted in reverie.

"Well since we're all sharing," Boudreaux said impatiently, "Gnome, why don't you explain where you got those nasty welts on your face, and then I'll tell everyone about my cheery reunion with our friend Ruprecht."

They shared their stories over Arden's surprisingly tasty gruel. Ohlen seemed somehow to be regaining strength by the minute. It was Boudreaux's story that seemed to leave them all in the deepest state of consternation.

Gnome summed up, "So X'andria saw some evil guy by Fish City and now she's gone off somewhere, Ohlen was attacked by a dead monster, I got mugged by Rove and his idiots, and our dear friend Ruprecht watched as his friend cooked Boudreaux in the street. That's quite a few days we've had."

"So what do we do?" Arden asked eagerly.

"I think we begin with a visit to Ruprecht and Dortmund," replied Ohlen evenly. "We know where they are likely to be, and they just might have some answers."

"Excellent," breathed Boudreaux cracking his knuckles. He pushed himself slowly back from the table.

It was the best idea he had heard in a while.

Ohlen's gaze immediately fixed upon the human skull.

Chapter Twenty
THE TEMPLE

_____

What a thrill! The warm night air crackled with power and possibility.

Dortmund had never felt so alive, so totally in control, so completely focused.

He had shown that big stupid oaf. All his practice was paying off. And he had shown Ruprecht his might, too. _Ruprecht will follow me to the ends of the earth,_ he thought smugly.

But there was so much more work to do. This power was just the beginning of his glorious ascent. Dortmund inhaled deeply through his nose, filling himself up with the smell of Rockmoor at midnight. Of his city. He lengthened his strides and smiled.

"You see, Ruprecht, what happens when people cross me?"

He sauntered down the lit stone streets of Hillcrest now.

"It doesn't matter their size," he prattled on airily, "because my power comes from above."

He turned the corner to the temple.

"And someday I'll share some of it with you, too, Ruprecht, when you're ready."

He stopped and turned to Ruprecht, but Ruprecht was nowhere to be found.

"Ruprecht?"

"With our deepest respect, sir, we wish to speak with one of your brethren." *How did Ohlen learn to be so damn charming?* Boudreaux wondered to himself as Ohlen negotiated their visit at the temple.

"His name is Dortmund," Ohlen specified, in response to a murmured question Boudreaux could not make out from the back of the group.

Boudreaux watched the priest, or cleric, or whatever you called people in places like this, get a hard-to-read expression on his face. Like he was carefully crafting a response in his mind.

Boudreaux did not like this look. And he felt the taut fingers of impatience crawling up the backs of his legs. *Ten seconds,* he thought, *this robe gets ten seconds before he gets a taste of Boudreaux.*

The robed man disappeared. Ohlen turned to the group and whispered simply, "He is checking."

The temple was a beautiful place. Made of bright white stone, it had high arched ceilings flooded by light from unseen windows that gave the entire space an ethereal glow. Each of the alcoves had ornate carved friezes surrounding a single life-size statue depicting some wonderful or horrible rapturous experience.

X'andria would love to see this, Boudreaux thought sourly.

The man shuffled back into view, this time bringing a friend. Both were dressed in simple, scratchy-looking brown robes and bore looks of pained consternation.

"What has he done?" The first man asked furtively. Overhearing this juicy snippet of the hushed discussion, Boudreaux had to bite his tongue not to spoil the whole serene civilized-conversation-thing Ohlen was so good at creating.

Moments later, they left the sanctuary and headed back out into the muggy grey drizzle of mid-afternoon.

"He is not part of the brotherhood at all," Ohlen explained as he led them purposely around the corner of the enormous building. "Dortmund is the groundsman and caretaker here."

"How strange," Arden gave voice to the combination of head-shaking and audible exhalations from both Gnome and Boudreaux.

"Apparently we can visit him through a separate entrance around the back."

"Just a reminder, everyone," Boudreaux growled as they neared the wide wooden trap door covering the stairs to the caretaker's residence, "that even though this is Cleaning Boy, he packs a nasty sting when he touches you."

Boudreaux hoisted the door from the ground as though it were weightless, and Arden took the lead down into the musty gloom below.

It was dark.

"Gnome?" Arden whispered.

Chapter Twenty

Two seconds and several mutters later, the cramped space was brightened by several small, revolving balls of light.

"Whoa," said Arden. They were in a dirt basement. Above them was stone and silt, dewy from condensation or leakage or both. The walls were not smooth or linear, but more hollowed out of the earth like a partially-dug grave. Butts of candles lay strewn around the dank entry way, along with bits of discarded oddments long-forgotten outside the area of candle glow.

"Let's move," Boudreaux insisted, too loudly, from the rear of the party.

They advanced along. Numerous cobwebby corridors shot off in all directions, but Arden stuck to the most well-traveled route.

Dortmund was agitating in his sleep when they came upon him. Gnome's brilliant light was virtually impossible to hide from, but in his dreamlike state Dortmund tossed and turned in an effort to shield his eyes.

The place was eerie. Jars and books were strewn along a makeshift table. Ohlen's gaze immediately fixed upon the human skull. And there were other harder to identify parts both human and animal.

"Ruprecht has been here, but I don't think he is now," Arden reported in a whisper, breathing deeply through his nose.

Dortmund was already stirring awake when Boudreaux ordered, "Get up, Dorton, it's time to talk."

Dortmund's jet-black hair was a mess. His sallow pock-marked features glowed in Gnome's light like an albino worm pulled from the earth that was never meant to see the sun.

"Wh-who's there? You get outta here," Dortmund spat defensively, somewhere between a startled whine and a desperate command. "Get out, this is my room, you're not allowed here." His eyes were still adjusting and so he was squinting them almost completely shut, with a pasty hand held up to shield his face from Gnome's omnipresent light.

"Put this on," Gnome spat back, and threw Dortmund his robe.

"We need you to tell us where Ruprecht is, Dortmund, it is important we speak with him." Ohlen had a slightly urgent, *let me handle this guys*, kind of edge to his voice.

"I'm not answering anything to anybody," Dortmund pouted. "You get out of here. You're not allowed in here."

Shooting a warning look at Boudreaux, Ohlen continued calmly, "We know you are a friend of Ruprecht's, Dortmund. We are also his friends and we would like to speak with him. If you tell us where he is, we will leave you in peace."

At this, Boudreaux gave Ohlen a *like hell we will* eyebrow raise, but kept his mouth shut.

"I don't know where Ruprecht is," Dortmund whined. "He was with me last night, but that's the last I saw of him. Somewhere between Westwood and here he disappeared."

"Somewhere in Westwood when you boiled me in the street with some stupid trick, you mean," Boudreaux couldn't contain himself any longer and advanced forward.

"Hey, what's this?" Gnome had crawled above them all, across the ceiling, and was upside down like a lizard on the far wall, by the table, pointing at a faint fissure in the dirt floor.

Dortmund jumped awkwardly into the air with a terrified look on his face. "Y-you stay away from that!" he shrieked. "You don't touch my things—you'll regret you ever came here—get out before I make you all sorry."

Boudreaux lunged like a lion into the space between Dortmund and Gnome. "Open it, Gnome, let's see what dark things Dorty is hiding here in his dark hole."

"Don't you touch that," Dortmund squealed and he reached for Boudreaux's enormous forearm.

Boudreaux saw the action unfold before it actually happened. He swung a closed fist down on top of the pale outstretched hand with such force and speed that he could feel bones in Dortmund's hand and forearm give way and shatter in mid-air. The howl that followed was punctuated by the loud crunch of Dortmund's right leg as Boudreaux pivoted and extended his heel through the space formerly occupied by his shin and ankle.

The whole thing took a second or two. Boudreaux had made only two swift motions, and again stood still in space, allowing the energy of his strikes to settle into the earth.

With his leg akimbo and bleeding from a compound fracture, and his broken hand cradled close to his chest, Dortmund was a heaving, sobbing mess on the floor.

"That is more than enough, Boudreaux," Ohlen sighed, frustrated.

"Eww! Look in here, guys," Gnome, stifling a gag, was still inverted on the wall above Dortmund's now-open trap door. "From all the bones in here, it looks like Dortmund's been leading a rich interior life of either grave robbery or butchery."

"WHAT IS HAPPENING HERE?" a huge deep voice demanded from the corridor behind them. It rang so loudly it made their ears hurt.

Striding into the space was a cleric, dressed all in white with a big brown beard, and large brown eyes open wide with fierce anger.

Dortmund continued to shake on the floor, but became totally silent.

The cleric took in the scene, and all their faces, with a single sweeping glance, but his narrowed eyes came to focus like pinpoints on a shiny object illuminated in the hole Gnome had uncovered in the floor.

"The crown that Elgar the Wise was buried in," the cleric's astonished voice had diminished to normal human proportions.

"Is your business with Dortmund complete?" he demanded of the room at large.

"Yes," answered Ohlen, at the same time that Boudreaux said, "No."

"Boudreaux," Ohlen looked at the big man meaningfully, "Dortmund is a powerless simpleton. He told us all he knows of Ruprecht. These things I know to be true. We are finished here."

"THEN GO!" The cleric commanded, his voice reverberating again from the air all around them.

The last they heard was Dortmund whimpering unintelligibly as the cleric lamented, "Oh, Dortmund, what have you done?"

When they left the temple grounds, the afternoon was darker, the wind blew, and rain fell lightly but persistently from ominous grey clouds.

They walked in silence, stewing in their own minds, over all they had just witnessed.

With no other plan, they proceeded back toward Westwood along the slick stone streets of Hillcrest.

Until Gnome motioned for them to stop. He dashed off the road, and they all followed like they were his shadows.

"We're not alone," Gnome informed them.

*She regained consciousness slowly through a thick
heavy fog, and almost immediately regretted it.*

Chapter Twenty-One
TO THE SEA

"What is it, Gnome?" whispered Arden.

They were huddled together partway down a narrow alley between two large and sturdy stone buildings. Rain came insistently now, and a growing stream of runoff from the sprawling stone that paved most of Hillcrest was rushing down the alley around their feet on its way toward lower ground and the sea beyond.

"Someone's a few streets behind us, tracking our movement," Gnome answered in a low voice.

Drops of water landed on his face and in his eyes as he squinted up at his friends. "You three go on. I'll stay here. With any luck, I'll be able to surprise them, or at least learn what we're dealing with and catch up with you back at the cottage."

So Ohlen, Arden, and Boudreaux emerged back onto the main

street. The rain had driven any would-be pedestrians indoors, and the thick clouds muted whatever was left of twilight. They turned toward Westwood, but stayed close together to obscure the fact that Gnome was no longer in their midst.

They had not gone far before they heard the tussle.

Gnome had flown off the wall, from a vantage point about ten feet in the air, onto the unsuspecting pursuer. They were rolling and grappling in the street like two tomcats fighting over the same territory.

Racing back, they saw that Gnome was entwined with an assailant not much bigger than himself. Boudreaux stepped in, pulled the two apart, and held the thin young man aloft by the collar of his tunic.

He was sputtering, "M-mister Gnome, Mister Gnome, it's me Waif."

"Waif!" cried Boudreaux setting the terrified young man back down on his feet. Gnome stood up dirty and sopping wet. "*This* is what saved you from a swim in the Torrent a few nights ago, Gnome?" Boudreaux pointed and laughed heartily. "They don't make you thieves very big, now, do they?" He was amused, in spite of the scowl Gnome leveled at him.

"Sorry I jumped you, Waif," said Gnome, panting slightly. "Are you hurt?"

"I'm fine, Mister Gnome," Waif returned tremulously. "I'm just a bit winded. I ran here all the way from Fish City."

Waif instantly had their full attention.

"How did you know where we were, Waif?" Ohlen gently asked the question on all of their minds.

"Oh," Waif looked down at his feet and said simply, "I have friends, sir."

A moment or two passed in which falling rain was the only sound. They were all still looking at him expectantly, so the young thief hurriedly continued. "When Mister Gnome asked me about the docks, it seemed really important." Here Waif paused a moment, before turning to Gnome and confessing, "So I asked some friends to follow you, Mister Gnome, so if I found something, I'd be able to get to you fast."

"What'd you find, Waif?" Boudreaux asked bluntly.

Waif looked nervously over his shoulder. "I asked about the tattooed sailors," he said in a low voice. "I asked a man who knows things, who knows what happens when night falls in Fish City. I lied to him." Waif was whispering now, "I told him The Master wanted to know." There was fear in the boy's eyes.

"What did he tell you?" Ohlen pressed lightly.

"Nothing, sir. He didn't say anything about the sailors. At least not with his mouth. He just looked really annoyed, and then said that me and The Master should mind our own business in The Grotto and leave the sea to the sailors." Waif's voice was barely a hiss. "But I saw him look out at the water, down a ways southward of the docks. So I said I was sorry for bothering him and left fast. But after a little while I snuck back to the seaside, down by where he looked." They were all leaning in close, as the young rogue concluded in an excited breath, "And I found something!"

"Good work Waif!" Gnome encouraged. "What was it?"

"I'm not sure exactly, Mister Gnome, but I can take you there if you like. It's like a hole in the seawall. I hid and watched for a little while, not sure what I was seeing. And just as I was getting ready to leave, something came out of it, fast. It was big. I don't know if it was an animal or a man, but I've been running ever since." Waif was smiling sheepishly now, clearly proud of himself.

Chapter Twenty-One

And so they followed Waif. He darted through dark alleys, muddy slums, and hidden paths. On they sped from Hillcrest through Watertown and then down into the mud of the Grotto. At last, in the dark of night, they approached the storm-addled sea and the loudly crashing waves on the rocky coast to the south of Fish City.

Rain pounded down in sheets now, soaking them to the bone.

She couldn't see.

She regained consciousness slowly through a thick heavy fog, and almost immediately regretted it. Her body was burning. She felt scorched clear to the backs of her eyeballs. Movement caused her blistered skin to feel like it would split right open and let her bones pop out like a roast bird's.

Are my eyes open? she wondered. *I think they are.*

She forced her hand to probe the space immediately around her. It felt like cold, wet earth. It actually felt good on the burning skin of her fingers. She clawed some of the earth into a small ball and smeared it on her arm. The relief from the searing hot pain was significant.

For several minutes she worked, gingerly at first, to cover all her exposed parts with the thick mud, if that's what it was. She even rolled over and worked the cold slimy salve into her scalp and ears and neck and ever so gently, her eyelids.

Never in her life had X'andria so appreciated the simple absence of pain.

The roiling sea itself came into view through the slanting rain. It swirled angrily—like some huge titan had stirred the inky blackness into a frenzy.

Chapter Twenty-Two
THE SEAWALL

Waif cautiously slowed their pace as they emerged from the Grotto into the southern edge of Fish City. The low-slung buildings, temporary stalls, and makeshift sea shacks offered much less in the way of cover from prying eyes than the huddled mud tenements they had threaded their way through in The Grotto.

As far as they could tell, though, the area was deserted. The driving rain must have sent the sailors and dockhands scurrying for cover in the seedy Fish City bars or rocking boats in the harbor.

The moon was hidden by a thick blanket of clouds hanging ominously overhead. The docks to the north of them were somewhat protected by an ancient breakwater surrounding the harbor, but here, unhindered, the massive waves crashed into the seawall, causing spray that exploded up and out of sight into the night.

They crept to the steep tumble of boulders that made up the coast here, and the roiling sea itself came into view through the slanting rain. It swirled angrily—like some huge titan had stirred the inky blackness into a frenzy.

Gnome felt nauseous. He did not like any form of water outside of a drinking skin. He hated being wet and had an unnatural fear of swimming at any depth. But this was like a nightmare. The waves were loud, menacing, and very, very wet. Even worse for Gnome, however, was the sight of the huge rolling mass of the sea beyond. The deceptively slow undulation of impenetrable mystery daunted him like little else.

"What are we looking at, Waif?" Boudreaux shouted over the pounding rain and crashing waves. Ohlen had fallen to one knee and placed a hand on the nearest boulder. Arden squinted down toward the water.

Waif pointed at the rocks below. "It's hard to see at night from here, sir," he shouted back, wind whipping his thin face, "but do you see that big rock jutting out right there? The opening is just under it."

Either he had not heard them, or he was pretending not to, but Gnome just stood there with his eyes squeezed tightly shut, as if hoping it was all a bad dream.

"Is that water coming out of it?" Arden yelled, to no one in particular.

"Looks like it," replied Boudreaux, squinting now himself. "Must be seawater washing back out."

Arden turned, "Is that what you saw coming out of there, Waif? Water?"

"No, sir," protested Waif. "What came out had legs, sir."

A moment or two passed.

"Well, I guess we should go down and check it out then," groused Boudreaux. "It doesn't look like easy going, though, and it'd be one hell of a night for a fall into the drink."

Gnome came to life. "I'm not going down there," he said staunchly.

"None of us want to go down there, Gnome," Ohlen's rich baritone emanated through the elements, "but go down we must."

Waif, Boudreaux, Gnome and Arden all turned to Ohlen as he struggled to his feet. Ohlen, his white cape flowing around him, seemed somehow to be clean and almost dry, unaffected by the torrential wind and rain swirling around them.

"But..." Gnome began.

"She's here, Gnome," Ohlen explained firmly. "X'andria is here, and so are others held against their will. We must venture within."

Normally so fleet of foot, Gnome felt like every step might be his last as they picked their way down the craggy, sea-soaked descent toward the mysterious opening. All his lessons had abandoned him. *See through the skin of your fingers and toes*, The Master had said. *Your hands are liquid, your feet are jelly* was another common refrain. But Gnome was too distracted—glancing nervously below at the churning froth—to employ his training this night.

And then there were the rats. Rockmoor had plenty: they could be found scavenging beneath the boardwalks of Westwood, rooting through trash in the alleys of Hillcrest and Watertown, swimming in the filthy Torrent River, and scampering all over the Grotto. But here, it seemed as if the wall was made partially of rock, and partially of rat. And so with every shaky grip and every tentative step, another huge furry body was dislodged squeakily from its dark, wet hiding place.

Boudreaux led the way. Having himself been imprisoned more

than once, he knew that every moment counted for X'andria.

Boudreaux was also the first to nearly slip and fall into the watery depths. Naturally, he blamed the rat. One moment he was methodically stepping, stretching, and groping his way along, and the next he found himself face to face with the giant varmint. *Man, they make them big around here!* he thought as the glowing eyes in the rocky crack before his face raced toward him to reveal the enormous body they belonged to.

The rat hissed at him. At least that's how he interpreted the noise it made. Most rats seemed scared of people, but this one appeared more annoyed than anything else. Seeing the rat was not the direct cause of Boudreaux nearly falling into the sea. The rat's rapid approach toward his face, however, did cause him to lose focus and place his left foot on a patch of glistening algae, from which it slid instantly. The next thing he knew, Boudreaux was hanging precariously, holding on with the fingers of just one hand while his body, heavy with armor and weaponry, swayed dangerously over the hungry waves below.

The opening was larger than they thought it would be. The boulder protruding above it provided a very effective camouflage for what now appeared to be a man-made entrance. It was large enough that Boudreaux and Arden had only to stoop to gain passage.

It smelled bad.

Even with the cleansing rain and crashing waves and gusty winds, the odor snaked its way into their awareness before they actually entered. Mixed, as it was, with the fishy, salty mélange of the sea, only Arden recognized the smell right away.

"Is this a sewer?" he exclaimed breathlessly as soon as he arrived on the landing. Arden was in the rear of the group, so they were all standing on the relatively flat and firm footing when he swung down to join them and made this helpful pronouncement.

"Is that what's flowing out of here?" Gnome asked incredulously, looking down at the liquid running several inches deep around his ankles and over his precious eel-skin slippers. Whatever it was, it dribbled down the shelf of rock behind them before being lapped away into oblivion by the waves.

"Let's get on with this," Boudreaux urged.

At one time there had been a grate. But all that was left were rusty nubs where the bars had long been torn asunder.

In spite of himself, Gnome sloshed forward into the vile opening. The smell was overwhelming, but almost as soon as he was within, and the imminent danger of falling to a watery death was behind him, his wits returned. So too, with earth and rock above him, began to prickle his natural senses for depth and terrain underground.

He was just starting to feel stable when he was shoved unexpectedly from behind. Gnome sailed face-first into the trickling stream of foul filth.

"Gnome? Was that you? Sorry, I can't see anything in here," Arden was trying to explain as Gnome extricated himself slowly from the sludge, dripping frustration, and who knows what else.

"You should go back, Waif. This is not your fight," Gnome murmured gravely as they plodded on through the shallow murky stream.

After the unfortunate shoving and falling incident, Arden had—with some effort—lit a torch from his leather field satchel. With each spark from the flint, uncanny reflections jumped all around them. It seemed that tiny mirrors, or little jewels, made up the walls and ceiling of the cramped tunnel, and even floated along by their feet. Seconds before the torch sputtered to life, Boudreaux realized that all the bright little spots were, in fact, in pairs. They were not jewels at all, of course: they were eyes.

The rats did not scatter instantly out of fear, like some do when surprised by light and large presences. They slunk away, but their gait was a slow amble, more out of preference for dark than fear. One particularly large beast tarried longer than the others, and seemed to size up the five interlopers, as if calculating its odds, before scurrying deeper into the blackness before them.

"I'm staying with you, Mister Gnome," the boy's voice trembled back through the half-light. His leather sling swung gently like a limp tail from his right hand; in his left, he had hefted an oblong stone bullet from a bag he wore around his waist.

After several minutes, the compact round drainage tunnel they were wading through opened abruptly into a large sewer main. The expanse was covered by a slow-moving dark liquid of unknown depth. Thankfully, running along the far left wall was a narrow elevated path.

The footpath did not connect to the drainage tunnel through which they'd entered. There were four or five feet separating the slimy, semi-filled mouth of the drainage tunnel from the end of the footpath. The level of the path was also slightly higher than the drain.

Boudreaux jumped.

It was not a graceful leap, and he landed with a noisy clatter of metal on stone, but somehow Boudreaux managed to keep his footing.

Waif was next in line. "Throw him, Arden," Boudreaux called,

"I'll get him."

The young rogue's eyes widened as he took in the expanse of muck separating him from his destination. Arden passed the torch he was holding to Ohlen, and maneuvered awkwardly to get his hands under Waif's armpits for the toss. Lacking room to move, however, he had to edge his way to the grimy lip of the tunnel, so his elbows could protrude into the dank air of the sewer main. Waif's feet were dangling over the muck. Realizing the direction things were going in, Waif hastily tucked his sling and bullet back into his bag, and had just managed to buckle it securely when, with a grunt, Arden launched him into space.

All things considered, it was a pretty good toss. The power was definitely sufficient, and the alignment was even true. But Waif, in anticipation of landing, adjusted his body into a pike position so that his feet would land first. This made it difficult for Boudreaux to get a clean hold on his upper body.

Waif's feet did, in fact, connect with the path, but his backside was so far behind him, that he could not stabilize. Instinctively he threw his hands out toward Boudreaux, who grabbed hold of them like an iron vise. But Waif's feet slipped from the path and he dipped, waist deep, into the disgusting cesspool beneath. Boudreaux quickly pulled him out, but the damage was already done.

"Whew! That is really gross," Boudreaux exclaimed as he deposited the whimpering thief on the path beside him. "Now at least we have a sense how deep this thing runs."

"You ready, Gnome?" Arden asked with as much enthusiasm as he could muster.

"It'll be the last thing you ever do," Gnome growled dangerously. And he disappeared upward around the edge of the tunnel, slithering like an enormous salamander while the others watched in amazement.

Arden and Ohlen each leapt and landed, with a little steadying from Boudreaux, without incident.

The path forward seemed firm. At odd intervals, they passed holes of varying sizes and differing heights, some of which deposited copious amounts of rainwater into the sewer main, while others were dry or dribbling.

After several minutes, with Arden and his torch in the lead, they came upon a stone staircase leading upward. Arden stopped and turned to his companions with a questioning look. But he found himself staring beyond them, instead, eyes wide. The others turned to follow his gaze.

Rats pursued them. Staying just beyond the range of the torchlight, there must have been hundreds of them. But these creatures were even larger than those they had encountered in the drainage tunnel, and they were much, much larger than those outside on the seawall. These were the size of small dogs, and their intelligent eyes burned with hungry intent.

Unable to control himself, Boudreaux raced at the nearest of the rats, to kick and stomp on them, or scare them away. In perfectly choreographed waves, however, they slipped noiselessly off the ledge into the murky black sludge as he approached. This would have been satisfying, had they not quickly scuttled back up onto the path behind the newly exposed forward ranks. Feeling foolish, Boudreaux skulked back to the party, as the rats filled in methodically behind at a safe distance.

"Should we go up?" Arden asked hopefully.

"Up takes us to street level," answered Ohlen. "X'andria and the others are that way." He pointed forward along the path.

"Would have been nice to know about *this* entrance," Gnome

muttered as they passed the stair and continued onward.

Not only were the rats huge, they were fast, ferocious, and seemed to be all sharp teeth and claws when they attacked. For the most part, they were not terribly difficult to kill or wound mortally, but there were just so many that when they finally ambushed the party, it was hard to defend against the multifarious onslaught.

The attack began from two of the dry drain holes. The party was walking by when Waif suddenly shrieked, a grey, furry body clamped bloodily onto his left forearm. Gnome, lightning fast, drove and twisted his dagger lethally into the squirming body, which caused it to release the shocked Waif from its jaws. Gnome hefted the twitching hairy mass into the sludge behind him, but the shrieks of battle were already echoing from all sides.

Boudreaux had been itching for engagement. His heavy protective gear made him a difficult target for claws and teeth. Rather than use weapons, he elected to stomp and grab and twist and throw. Broken bodies slid and flew from him in all directions like he was a human tornado. The few nips that landed between his plates only spurred him on to more fury. He was so successful, in fact, that from the rear of the party, his progress through the attackers separated him slightly from the others as he pounded his way back toward the staircase they had passed just minutes before the attack.

Waif was struggling. He had a knife in his right hand, but the shock and pain of bite on his other arm had left him disoriented and slow. The rats were low targets, and it was all he could do to kick and stab feebly to protect his skinny exposed legs.

Chapter Twenty-Two

Thank goodness for Gnome, though. Low to the ground, spinning like a dervish, Gnome's dagger slashed through the air with awe-inspiring speed and precision. Gnome's personal mission was to see Waif safely back above ground, and he stayed near his charge, methodically dispatching one threat after another. He was particularly grateful for the ornate dwarven bracers still fitted tightly around his forearms, making his lethal appendages nearly impervious to the savage claws and teeth slashing and gnashing all around him.

Ohlen sensed evil here: it lay beyond, deeper into the unknown. Rats were survivors. Killers. Merciless in their drive for self-preservation. But they were not evil. Not the kind of brooding, calculating, sadistic evil that Ohlen knew awaited them.

This current fight consisted, therefore, of tactics and steel. Ohlen had engaged several of the filthy dripping critters, when he noticed Arden struggling to hold his torch aloft while wielding the shorter of his two weapons.

"Arden," Ohlen shouted, taking some clawed damage to his legs as he raced to his companion undefended, "let me take that!" and he wrested the torch free from Arden's grasp.

Taking his second blade to hand, Arden became a mesmerizing windmill of whirring steel. He advanced forward, clearing the way before him like one might sweep dry leaves from a walkway. Cleaved slices of rat flew from his blades in all directions.

This was a turning point. With Boudreaux squishing, squeezing, and tearing three or four rats at a time in one direction, and Arden shredding his way through the other, Ohlen, Waif and Gnome were soon left with nothing to fight in the middle, apart from the occasional varmint swimming up from the sewer to scrabble over the ledge before them.

"Let's have a look at that bite," Gnome was saying to Waif, when they heard something totally unexpected.

The clang of steel on steel.

Turning to the sound, they saw that Arden was engaged in melee combat.

He was fighting some kind of abomination. On two legs, it was the size and shape of a small person, a bit bigger than Waif. It was covered with swirling wisps of grey hair, thicker in some places than others, and clutched a rusty short sword with a stubby clawed cross between hands and paws.

As the creature fought, it wheezed and grunted noisily. Its grey-pink mottled face was wrinkly and hairless apart from whiskers and tufts in and around its pointy ears. Long canine lips stretched around a row of razor-sharp teeth, bared in a perpetual snarl.

Arden was the superior swordsman by far. His blades danced and darted, and he landed blow after blow. With each cut and stab, the creature grunted and became more ferocious, but somehow it seemed largely unhurt. There was no blood, and it did not slow. Not once was it able to get through Arden's expert defenses with its sword, but occasionally it lashed out with a free claw and sliced at his face and chest.

Breathing heavily, rat-blood glistening on his fingers, Boudreaux clomped up behind Waif, Gnome, and Ohlen to see what all the ruckus was about. Three more of the horrid rat-people were now slinking up behind the one engaged with Arden. Arden was beginning to show signs of fatigue.

"Ugly bastards, aren't they," Boudreaux observed. "I'm gonna need to get by," he said matter-of-factly, as he pushed his way past the others on the narrow stone ledge.

Boudreaux leaned casually against the grimy wall behind the

struggling Arden.

"Nice technique, Arden!" he shouted amiably to his friend.

"What the hell?" Arden managed between lunges, "I've hit this thing enough times, it oughta be in little pieces by now."

"Want me to show you how it's done?" Boudreaux taunted, while the others looked on in horror.

"All yours, tough guy," Arden squeezed through gritted teeth, and he gave a powerful lunge to allow for time to shift positions.

Boudreaux pushed himself easily from the wall and reached over his head for the ornate short sword he had picked up in Bridgeton.

His first back-hand blow knocked the blade clean out of the grip of the beast that was holding it. He swung forward next, in a downward arc that separated its snarling elongated head from its body.

"The thing is, Arden," Boudreaux said conversationally over his shoulder as the second creature rushed forward to engage him, "and believe me, I learned this the hard way." He stopped talking for a moment, while he ended the second assailant with a powerful thrust just below its neck.

"You need silver for half-human freaks like this."

Arden, suddenly reflective, received this bit of sage wisdom with a mix of emotions.

Get them. The words ceaselessly beat like a drum in its head. Oblivious to the screams of the woman it passed on the street, heedless of the rain, it tracked the aura like a dog following a scent.

THE SEAWALL

They were just here. Not far now. Mutilated feet with missing toes slapped carelessly onto wet and pointy rocks. It did not feel its flesh being punctured here and there. The objective was all that mattered.

So close. The need urged it forward into the darkened tunnel, leaving the sea crashing behind.

*The tattoos began to swim. At first they swirled within
the skin in which they were drawn, the inky flames
flickering and writhing like black snakes.*

Chapter Twenty-Three
X'ANDRIA

The pain was becoming tolerable. Though possibly just a trick her nerves were playing on her, the cool wet mud she had painstakingly applied to her skin seemed to make a difference.

She had been in shock. All she could think about was the burning. What little energy her flummoxed mind could muster was frantically occupied with the search for relief.

Afraid to move, X'andria lay still, face down, and became aware of her breathing. The rising and falling of her back slowed down as she began to trust that the burning sensation was receding.

What happened to me? she finally allowed.

And then the blazing nightmare returned.

What had happened to her was bad, but what it meant—what it

triggered inside her—was far worse. She began sobbing convulsively, and the sudden movement caused her skin to scream again.

She had gone back to the docks, needing to know if he was there. She had seen one of those terrible fiends. She had wanted to spy on them, to see how many there were, to see which boat was theirs. To see if it was the *same one.*

She had crept through the night. The time was well after midnight, but the sky had been clear and the various creaking and swaying manmade contraptions of wood and rope were illuminated by the lunar glow. A ramshackle stall, with two open sides, had stood near the place she had seen the Islander.

The stall had reeked with layer upon layer of dried fishy juices left over from countless mornings of gutting, scaling, shucking, and hocking slippery creatures that had been hauled up from the depths of the sea. She had pictured them, mouths working in the suffocating air, eyes staring blankly at the alien world, all the elegance and color of their scintillating undersea lives stripped from them in their final moments.

And it reminded her of the little girl.

The girl was cowering in the corner, eyes brimming with tears, but afraid even to cry. Crying was discouraged. It was punished. And she quickly learned to hold back the flood, somehow balancing the heavy tears on her eyelids, somehow convincing her eyes not to make any more, chin jutted out just enough to give the impression of fortitude and defiance even though all she was trying to do was keep the wet sadness from running down her cheeks and exposing her weakness.

X'ANDRIA

They pulled her from her childhood. They reeled her away from the care and love and support and freedom and guidance and promise her mother had created so carefully around her. She tried to be good— she did what she was told to the best of her abilities. But it didn't matter.

The punishment came, she realized, not as a result of her actions but because of their sickness. Their character, softened by opulence and corrupted by power, left them weak with false superiority. So they took out their frustrations on their slaves, on the kids, on the little girl.

At first she lived under the delusion that it was all some terrible mistake. That it was temporary. That soon she would be discovered. That her mom would come for her and that she would be liberated. But months passed, and slowly her youthful hope eroded. Her imagination, once such a bright and limitless haven, became no less vivid, but far more desolate.

That was the worst. There was no longer any escape. No place to hide. No place to dream. No place to forget. She arrived at a crossroads rarely visited by one so young and from which few ever return: hopelessness.

She served the fat man. She brought him things to eat and drink. Her world during the day was the kitchen, with brief sojourns to whatever part of his sprawling seaside villa he happened to be luxuriating in. He was rarely alone. Usually he had guests: imposing men with hatred and lust barely contained beneath a veneer of cordiality. The fat man had power and money, and X'andria could sense they wanted both, and they wanted more.

He was outside lounging, under a broad-leafed squat tree. Nearby was a rock-rimmed salty swimming pool fed by the sea. She had olives, but he was angry. The fat man did not yell often, but today he was in a towering rage. One of his visitors stood stone-faced before him, venom and defiance in his eyes, while two of the huge tattooed Islanders looked on with folded arms. She lingered with her olive plate, unsure what to do.

The fat man made a limp gesture with the fingertips of his left hand. The Islander on that side stepped forward, pulling off the loose white tunic that covered the ornate swirls of flame all over his body. The visitor lost the hard edge of his glare to uncertainty.

The tattoos began to swim. At first they swirled within the skin in which they were drawn, the inky flames flickering and writhing like black snakes. But then they jumped from his body in a blaze of fiery orange and red, like he was a human torch. Flaming torrents tumbled forward engulfing, then roasting the terrified visitor.

At some point during the swirling, during the screaming pleas and the hideous immolation, the olives dropped from her tiny hands. The earthenware platter exploded. The olives rolled away like little traitors abandoning a losing battle. The charred man had not yet stopped twisting on the ground when she was hefted over the shoulder of the other Islander like a sack of grain, and shuttled wordlessly to a small, lightless underground chamber she had never seen before.

And there she stayed.

She was trembling from the shock of what she had just seen. There was no explanation for it. The cold cruelty was unimaginable. The fiery animation of the tattoos was terrifying. And the black void of hopelessness inside her became tinged with fear for her very survival. It was the worst night of X'andria's life.

But one night was not all she spent in that hole with only her fears and imagination for company.

Over and over again she vividly recalled the execution. She saw the flames in her mind's eye. While at first the flames were a source of fear, soon she realized that they brought something else to her as well.

The flames brought light and color back to the drab bleakness into which her dreams had shriveled. The impossibility of their existence became a new source of wonder. If fire can be drawn on skin, and called upon at will, then what else is possible? And so as time passed in solitude, her imagination began to flourish. She began to hope again.

She began to dream. Of escape.

Why had she followed him? After a long night and an even longer day camped uncomfortably in that fishy stall she had seen him. He had been carrying a large crate along the dock when she had spotted the tattooed man again from her hiding place. *A crate large enough for a little girl,* she had thought bitterly. That was why she had followed.

He had turned and walked purposely along the coast, and she snuck after him. He had disappeared around a corner. She had tarried a moment, followed him, and then she had walked into blinding light as bright as the sun.

And she had awoken here. In pain, alone, in the dark. It was like all those years of freedom never happened. Like her escape, her time on the streets with the urchins and thieves and Gnome, her prodigal consumption of language and magic with The Alchemist, her friendships—all was a dream snatched from her and burned up in the blink of an eye. She had become the scared little girl again.

The girl without hope.

In spite of the pain, X'andria lifted her arms to hug herself and murmured softly the one comfort she could think of: *laamnu neila hiiwa.* Sleep little one.

A slumped oily sack growing from the ground, the smooth onyx had given way to a wrinkly mound of moist jet-black flesh with two burning eyes above a sunken, toothless mouth.

Chapter Twenty-Four
HUNGER

It was almost always hungry now. So he was almost always hungry too. The perfect onyx image he had fashioned into the floor had changed. It had grown.

It mutated with each feeding. For weeks just a voice inside his head helping and directing him, in the last two days it had become a constant gnawing presence reigning over his mind.

All the studying, scheming, secret-stealing, and planning by candlelight had led to the glorious moment when its eyes blazed for the first time. All the fear, all the hard work, the blood, the death, was worth it in that first moment they locked together. His mom would have been proud.

Chapter Twenty-Four

It was more than he could have imagined. Of course it was. How could any human conceive of the enormity of the gods? None could. *Until now.*

The book had come to him months ago. It had been sent to him. He was meant to have it.

After years of dark deals, favors for secrets, and services in exchange for curiosities, he had found Jastro. The big merchant brought questionable things into Rockmoor from time to time, and questionable things were just what he was after.

One night they met in the back of their usual Watertown bar. Jastro had a smug look on his face as he wiped ale scum from his lips with the back of his hand. The fat bastard had clearly found something special and was looking to deal.

The following night on the docks, with nearly all he had of value loaded into a chest, he remembered saying desperately, "This had better be everything you say it is, Jastro, or..."

"Or what?" Jastro had chortled. "You'll swim after me and spit water at my hull?"

The expressionless tattooed Islanders surrounding the fat man had turned with him to board the vessel. "Enjoy your new toy, I hope you'll use it as well as I would," Jastro called, still laughing, as he disappeared onto the deck.

The rough wooden crate had been heavy in his arms as he carried it slowly back to The Grotto. He had to stop and put it down many times to rest his arms and catch his breath. Finally he had stolen into the hidden door and his stairs beyond that led down into the bowels of the city. In dim candlelight, surrounded only by his darkest treasures, he pried open the lid and plunged his fingers into the cool, scintillating, silver-clear fabric of the cloak Jastro had promised would make him invisible. His heart raced.

Imagine what I can do, if no one can see me, he thought.

The glistening fabric had fallen through his fingers like shimmering sheets of the purest water. Extracting the magnificent garment from the crate, he struggled to figure out how to put it on. On his feet, ears pounding with exhilaration, he could hardly wait to try out his new prize in The Grotto brothels.

Then something else in the crate caught his attention: a small black tattered book. In spite of his obsession with the cloak, he had stalled, intrigued by the surprising discovery. He bent and extracted it from the crate and sat briefly to peek inside the cover. It was not a large book, but he sat transfixed, immobile, dressed in his invisible cloak, for two full days. He got up only to light new candles when the old ones guttered. And when next he ventured above ground, he was a barely noticeable ripple in light, a ripple in search of a slab of onyx and two red rubies.

The pathway to the power of The Gaoler, he had since learned, was through suffering. Every acquisition and every preparation must bathe in the blood and tears of loss and pain. His task had been to fashion a demon likeness from materials collected and hewn by violence. *Blood,* the book demanded, *spilled in anguish,* was vital at every stage of invocation.

He had killed the shopkeeper for the precious stones.

Chapter Twenty-Four

It was an awkward and messy job, as he had never been good with a blade. Sneaking into the tidy Hillcrest shop late in the day, his cloak mimicking his surroundings like a chameleon, he had carefully perused the wooden boxes and shelves for the rubies and onyx he required. The book molded itself coolly to his skin through his breast pocket.

He was lousy at sneaking, and he made noises several times as he moved about the ancient shop. The old woman who owned the place, whose parents and parents' parents had owned it before her, ignored the first of the mysterious sounds. But soon she became suspicious, and her suspicion turned into fear.

Her fear was delicious to him. She retrieved a dusty club, untouched for years behind a shelf, and began stalking around the shop. The worry and strain emanating from her pores was sucked up thirstily by the book's pages and injected into him in the form of thrilling delight.

Onyx had been easy to find. The rubies were hidden in a more secure place, behind the purveyor's massive, marble-topped desk. Between the floor creaking and the gems clinking, the wiry crone raced to the sound and swung her club wildly in the air. It connected with surprising force with the side of his head.

And that blow was the first time he tasted the peculiar indulgence of pleasure at his own pain. He recoiled, dropping the rubies, his ears ringing and his face bleeding beneath the cloak. It hurt so badly, yet he wanted more at the same time.

In spite of his relative youth and the advantage of his invisibility, murdering the old woman required a prolonged sweaty struggle at the end of which myriad stones littered the floor around toppled wooden displays. When the grisly task was complete, he located and recovered the dropped rubies and stole back out of the shop, slipping gracelessly in the dark pool of blood expanding across the worn floor.

The book demanded the onyx be chipped with bone and polished with blood and strips of hide. When he ran out of blood, he sometimes supplied his own to whet its voracious appetite. Delirious from pain, ecstasy, and blood loss, he carved and polished for hours upon hours until he could sense the likeness was complete. His hands were raw, his muscles ached, he had killed, he had suffered, and almost as soon as he sat back to admire his work, the hunger for more began to needle and prod.

At last the eyes began glowing and his masterpiece began to speak to him. It directed him through elaborate preparations, to steal books from The Emporium, to create the servant monster out of Jastro's deckhand Mordimer, to recruit assistants to aid him in his ascension to glory. The rat-kind had come on their own. Finally, in recent days, The Gaoler's effigy had begun to feed and grow.

The Atolians were all gone. The Gaoler had sucked them dry one by one, and the Islanders stoically pitched their desiccated remains into the sewer.

It engorged itself with each feeding, and its distended mass could no longer be covered by the rug. A slumped oily sack growing from the ground, the smooth onyx had given way to a wrinkly mound of moist jet-black flesh with two burning eyes above a sunken, toothless mouth.

His arms were a patchwork of angry red scars and oozing wounds. With the Atolians gone, all that was left was that pathetic deckhand's family. But the tether he had placed on Mordimer's mind was inextricably linked to his love for his family. *They can't die, until he finishes his damn job.* The restriction was infuriating.

Hungry! The Gaoler screamed inside his head.

He dutifully reached for the black serpentine dagger he had used so many times before. No place remained on his arms. In desperation, his brain crushed by the insistence, he hoisted up his crimson robe and drew a short, deep line high on his left thigh.

Still holding the dripping blade, along with the heavy crimson folds of his robe, he stepped astride the shriveled horror on the ground and squatted to present his wound to the insatiable pursed lips. He was instantly rapt with unspeakable pain and magnificent ecstasy. It devoured his spirit as it drank of his blood, and the pleasure of sharing in the feeding was so great, he was unaware of his own tortured screams.

"Sir." If the Islander was surprised to see him squatting prone over the demonic mass, he did not betray it on his angular decorated face. "We have a new prisoner. A female."

The muted rhythmic scratching seemed so far away to X'andria as she replayed the horror of her childhood and stewed in the desperation of her predicament that it was awhile before she registered the sound.

When she finally did, she ventured a movement to investigate. First she brought her hands close to her side as if she might lift herself to a crawling position.

It didn't hurt!

It was miraculous. Slowly she pushed herself up onto all fours. Still no pain.

And finally X'andria's brilliant mind began whirring once more. She knew what had happened now. *Illusory corporeal manifestation.* Convince someone that something terrible is happening to them, and the mind and body will make it real. X'andria had not been burned, she had had the experience of being burned. And this knowledge made her a master over the illusion.

Crawling across the damp dirt floor toward the sound, she caught herself thinking, *When I get out of here, I must learn how to do that.*

She was at the stone wall now. The scratching continued.

"Hello?" she called, surprised at the strength of her own voice. "Is someone there?"

The scratching stopped abruptly.

"I'm X'andria, can you hear me?" She rapped on the stone with her knuckles. "Hello?"

"Zarina," a faint, forlorn voice replied. "I'm Zarina."

At least eight feet tall, its motions were slow but totally smooth, like the stone had somehow turned into animated molten tissue.

Chapter Twenty-Five
STONE AND STEEL

The rat-men were nimble and vicious. Lethal with swords, claws, or teeth and seemingly impervious to conventional weaponry, they were formidable opponents. But forced to fight one at a time on the narrow footpath against Boudreaux, who was armed with silver, their hybrid natural gifts were no match for his superior strength and combat skills.

The gleaming silver blade liquefied their flesh when he struck. A faint sizzle could just barely be detected beneath the high-pitched squealing that issued from their long crooked mouths with each devastating blow.

It did not take long for Boudreaux to finish off the two

remaining assailants. The last of the beasts was still sprawled on the path. He swiftly chopped off its head, before nudging the limp body into the murky river with his toe.

"Always good to take their heads off," he explained, looking at Waif and smiling darkly. "Halfies like these ugly bastards heal up quick and sometimes come back—unless the head's gone." He kicked the head off the ledge, too, for emphasis.

More of the sewer rats had been hovering nearby, but with the death of the fourth and final rat-man, the smaller cousins melted away into the filth.

"We are very fortunate for your knowledge of these beasts, for your skill, and for that silver." Ohlen intoned sincerely at Boudreaux. "Thank you."

Arden examined Waif. "That sure is a nasty-looking bite," he observed. "How are you feeling, how's the arm?"

Waif looked terrible. He was as white as a sheet and his skin glistened. Perhaps the sewer, the shock of it all, the pain and blood, the headless rat-man, or some combination had gotten to him. But Arden was suspicious of the bite. He poured some water from his skin over the torn flesh, and bound Waif's arm tightly with some fabric from his bag that he kept just for this purpose.

"Let's move," Gnome said grimly.

Arden's mind was like a catalogue of plants and animals of the natural world. One of his many gifts was pattern recognition, to the extent that he could follow even the faintest track. It was this gift that had spurred his sudden alarm at the unnatural destruction he had witnessed in the forest a few days earlier. It was this gift that told him now, without a doubt, that the passage to their left was the one to follow since it had seen the most foot traffic. And it was this gift that caused his blood to run cold and his spine to go rigid at the sight of organic matter bobbing beside them in the sewer, glistening in the flicker of the torchlight.

"What is that?" whispered Gnome, halting beside him and squinting after Arden's frozen gaze.

They had entered a wide junction where three large tunnels fed into a round pool. The way they had entered, it was clear from the flow, was the sole drainage line to the sea. In this domed room, the footpath widened to a more significant floor space surrounding the pool on all sides. Four narrow stone bridges arched over each of the slow moving streams. An open doorway, with large stone statues on either side, led into a dimly lit passageway to their left. The stench of the sewer seemed concentrated here, as if the dome distilled and fermented the foul stagnation beneath.

"I don't know," Arden whispered back. He wished that he were telling the truth.

"Looks like somebody shaved the hair off one of those rats," Boudreaux said. He was trying to use a low voice, though it did not quite come out that way.

"There are more floating beyond," Ohlen added, mournfully.

Waif doubled over and vomited. On his knees, trembling and sweating, the sick was down his front, on the stone floor, and mixed with the sludge over the edge.

Suddenly, from behind them sounded a bone-chilling rasp of stone grating on stone, and the floor shook violently beneath them. All but Waif wheeled around to see what had caused the thunderous noise.

Chapter Twenty-Five

Arden drew his sword instinctually even before he fully registered what his frantic nerves were scrambling to communicate. Gnome dashed like a phantom to Waif's crumpled form and began dragging him back toward the mouth of the drainage tunnel. Ohlen stretched his senses out in vain at the impossibility before them, but felt nothing beyond a cold empty void. Not always one with an eye for detail, it took Boudreaux a moment to figure out what exactly had happened.

One of the massive stone statues had moved.

It had stepped sideways, barring their passage into the space beyond, and now it was slowly turning its head as if taking stock of those trespassing before it. At least eight feet tall, its motions were slow but totally smooth, like the stone had somehow turned into animated molten tissue.

With its fingers curled into enormous club-sized fists, it took another thunderous step in their direction. It was with this step that Boudreaux's brain unfroze and helped him interpret the information his eyes were feeding him.

Without hesitation, Arden dropped his torch to the floor and charged the monstrosity. It was a good charge. Boudreaux had faced him day after day in training, but he had never seen the kind of speed-fueled power that Arden sunk into this charge. At the last moment he leapt into the air and swung his blade while twisting from his hips for maximum torque. The sword connected perfectly with the stone guardian's neck and the clang reverberated throughout the domed chamber. Arden landed nimbly just before its massive legs and rolled away as little bits of stone landed softly around him.

It was an excellent hit by any measure. But it did not seem to phase the living stone giant. The statue instead turned to face Arden, who was still gaining his balance, and raised its arms as if to strike.

The response came with surprising speed. Arden had hoped he would be able to dance around clumsy and lumbering movements. He was wrong. He just managed to slip beyond the first crushing blow, which came from above and ended with the monster's right fist embedded several inches into the stone floor beneath them. Arden's counter strike connected with the stone forearm, thick as a tree trunk, and this time sparks flew from the blade as it glanced awkwardly away.

Arden was expecting the stone giant to retract its right hand from the stone floor, because any organic being would have had to do that in order to muster the balance necessary for any kind of forceful assault. But this was no organic being. Even bent forward as it was, its left arm extended with astonishing speed at an impossible angle across its body.

Arden's finely honed reflexes allowed him to twist and evade the brunt of the blow. But the massive fist glanced off his breastplate, which was dented by the impact, and blew Arden off of his feet. He spiraled into the air and landed about ten feet away in a clatter of metal-encased limbs.

The horror stood erect and took several thunderous steps toward the splayed and immobile Arden before Boudreaux jumped atop it from behind, his colossal arms wrapped around its head in a choke hold violent enough to break the neck of a large bear.

The high-placed weight of Boudreaux's impact caused the monstrosity to pitch forward slightly and, for an instant, it appeared it might actually topple forward. But instead it stumbled and managed to stay upright.

To his disappointment, Boudreaux was reminded of the futility of trying to squeeze stone. He exerted the kind of phenomenal pressure few could manage on the huge head and neck, but there was no effect. Stone is virtually impossible to crush. It can, however, be broken or cracked, and some instinct in Boudreaux caused him to change tack and work toward separating the huge head from the massive neck and shoulders on which it rested.

That did not seem to be working either.

The main problem was leverage. Boudreaux did not have a good place to plant his feet to lift properly. He was just trying to sort that problem out, hanging from the head, feet scrabbling for purchase on the legs and waist, when the stone giant raised both arms over its head to hurl him from his perch.

The enormous thumbs forced their way beneath his armpits, and the thick fingers closed like four vise-clamps along the back of his rib cage. And it pulled, hard. Boudreaux tensed his body and his massive musculature, encased in armor plates, became almost as densely immovable as the statue itself.

Boudreaux's arms screamed, his shoulders nearly wrenched from their sockets, and the iron plates screeched and began to tear from the force.

The stone giant's second attempt at removal proved successful. It pulled Boudreaux from its back and hurled him like a doll onto the ground in front of it with bone-crunching fury.

But its head came off too.

Boudreaux's body was caked to the ground, like the monster had flung a big rotten tomato to splat on the floor. The huge stone head, still held tightly in his arms, came crushing down onto Boudreaux's chest at impact, and then rolled slowly off of him. It came to rest on its side, staring blankly ahead.

The grotesque statue was disoriented, but still very much animated. Arms swinging wildly in the air like the blades of a windmill, it kicked Boudreaux's prone form forcefully from the ground and launched him, fifteen feet or so, through the air.

Boudreaux's thoughts were coming very slowly. His armor had saved him from being pierced by the probing stone fingers. It had helped keep his arms attached during the extraction. Gasping for breath on his back, he even had the presence of mind to be thankful for the dwarf helmet that kept his head from cracking like an egg on the stone floor. And thinking of heads, he smiled weakly knowing he had actually yanked the statue's head off, with a little help from the statue itself.

He was slipping toward unconsciousness when it kicked him. Through his polished steel breast-plate, the jolt of the impact on the left side of his rib cage was enough to awaken him once more. And it was a good thing, too, because moments later he landed with a splurch in the middle of the cesspool and had just enough time for a gulp of putrid air, before his heavy armor tugged him beneath the surface of the thick sludge.

Boudreaux was sinking. Though normally a strong swimmer, the weight of his armor and gear made resurfacing completely hopeless. Eyes squeezed tightly shut to keep out the fetid slurry engulfing him, he flailed wildly before realizing his efforts were futile. He drifted further down into the thick fluid blackness. He was running out of air. An involuntary shudder caused a small amount of sewage to enter his nostrils, and only his most primal instincts for self-preservation kept him from throwing up and expelling the last of his precious breath in the process.

Frantically Boudreaux began stripping off his armor. He unbuckled the plates on his right arm, swallowing hard to assuage his body's desperate need for air. He then unbuckled and wrenched free his left arm, and immediately began slipping and sliding his breast-plate over his head.

Chapter Twenty-Five

Lungs burning, he lost control and opened his mouth to breathe. What rushed eagerly in was so vile, though, that it may have saved his life, because it instantly caused his jaw to involuntarily clamp shut again.

Boudreaux fell still further.

With all his gear stripped from his upper body, he tried to swim toward the surface. Disoriented, passing out, and without light, it was impossible for him to know if he was actually ascending, but Boudreaux knew he was out of time. With every ounce of strength and resolve available to him, he pulled himself up toward the surface.

The stone monstrosity began lumbering now toward Ohlen, Gnome, and Waif. Even headless, it appeared somehow to sense their presence. Arden was barely stirring against the far wall, and nothing more than bubbles on the surface of the vat of sewage signaled what was left of Boudreaux.

"I will distract it," Ohlen said solemnly, and he strode forward into the open space with his sword aloft.

The giant's power was immense. There was no contesting it, only evading the repeated crushing blows. Ohlen felt no spirit within the animated stone to befriend or turn or crush. In that way, it was not unlike the zombie fiend that had accosted him during his meditation.

Lacking a more comprehensive strategy, Ohlen focused on anticipating the giant's attacks, so that he might keep one step ahead, and stay alive.

Boudreaux erupted through the sludgy surface in a shower of sewage and bile. Gulping for air and sputtering, he thought his starved lungs might never feel full again. Keeping himself afloat despite the drag of his heavily laden legs, Boudreaux stabilized enough to take in the dire scene before him.

Ohlen was dancing around the huge headless stone guardian, narrowly avoiding crushing death with each maneuver. Arden was still recovering from the blow he had sustained, his torch flickering feebly on the ground in the middle of the space. Gnome seemed to be protecting Waif in the mouth of the drainage tunnel. *God help us if this thing touches one of them*, Boudreaux's mind was grinding slowly back into motion.

He began to swim. He reached the stone floor near Arden and slid messily out of the cesspool like he was one of the rats that lived here. In a glance he could see Ohlen was being forced closer and closer to the edge, and closer to Gnome and Waif as well.

Suddenly Boudreaux had an idea.

"Arden," he rasped, "the sewer!"

At the sight of Boudreaux emerging like a dripping swamp monster from the sludge, Arden snapped back to awareness.

"Now!" Boudreaux's voice was raw from the near-drowning and caustic juices.

Not entirely sure what to do, Arden moved to follow his friend, each step reminding him painfully of the damage his torso had just sustained.

Boudreaux's plan became clear soon enough. With Ohlen attracting the monster's wrath at the edge of the cesspool, Arden and

Boudreaux were able to crouch and lunge undetected at its huge stony backside. Ohlen skittered out of the way just in time, as the two powerful men poured every ounce of their strength into toppling the behemoth horror into the filth.

Halfway in, it began flailing its arms and kicking its legs in a frenzied dance of wild desperation. Its feet collided with the stone edge and cracked off large pieces of the floor before momentum carried them beyond. Still thrashing when it hit the surface of the sewage, it displaced a huge amount of the thick putridity and sprayed it in all directions. Soon enough, it sank heavily and hopelessly beneath the surface, leaving only a few viscous ripples in its struggling wake.

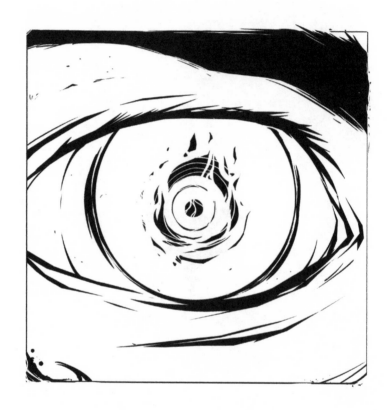

The glorious instant it had first seized him, its fire-red eyes installed themselves—perched just behind his own.

Chapter Twenty-Six
GOLD AND GRIME

The Gaoler never rested. It pushed his body and mind relentlessly to do its bidding. The cost was great, but the reward was greater.

Far, far greater.

The glorious instant it had first seized him, its fire-red eyes installed themselves—perched just behind his own. They had looked not only outward to see what he saw, but they also looked inward and absorbed all his memories. Two things had flashed before him. He saw the black book, and he saw the giant stone statues in the main sewer junction. The Gaoler had demanded that he bring the book before the statues.

He had obeyed. There was no question. He had no choice.

Chapter Twenty-Six

He had walked in the dark, with no need anymore for light, to the statue on the left. His knees buckled painfully, deliciously, to the ground before it, and he opened the book on the floor.

The pages were somehow different. He did not know the language of the book anymore, but somehow he was able to read it aloud anyway. The all-powerful presence in his mind devoured the information and unlocked its secrets at a rate that left his mortal mind spinning and his body heaving.

"Burn it," The Gaoler had commanded, after several hours.

He focused jets of white-hot flame from his fingertips onto the tattered pages. They leapt upward into an incendiary ball almost like they *wanted* to burn. In a few moments there was nothing left but smoldering ash.

Methodically, driven by otherworldly knowledge, He rubbed the ash all over the parts of the stone statue that he could reach. It awoke, and he felt it, too, perched inside his mind. He also felt the magical little book reform itself inside his breast pocket.

"Protect us," he demanded. "Stir when there are invaders, and crush them."

The cold stone consciousness had gone blank again.

Until this moment.

The tattooed Islander was lingering, as if awaiting a command. There was a new prisoner. A female prisoner. But now there were more pressing concerns. The stone giant had awoken.

With some effort—and more than a little regret—he stood, blackened blood dribbling down his left leg.

"We are breached," he said venomously. "Take your brethren to the junction and make the enemy suffer. Use your gifts to make sure they die slowly and painfully. We wish to feast on their misery."

The noise beyond was thunderous. There were shouts. *Was that Boudreaux's voice?* X'andria stood by the wall, totally alert. Her sharp eyes focused through the gloom and seized on a tiny shining object in the dirt.

My gold loop!

Whatever was happening outside, it was significant. Now was the time.

Clutching her gold loop close, she focused on the door. She focused on the latch that locked the door from the outside. Breathing steadily, slowly, she willed the latch to lift.

Her heart raced. *This is my chance,* she thought.

The door opened and X'andria sped into the hallway, looking quickly left to right. There were no guards. Zarina's cell was next to hers. X'andria was just about to open it when she noticed her belongings crumpled in a pile nearby.

Please, please, please, she begged as she rifled through the folds of her robes. *Yes, there it is!* Her silk bag of flint, parchment, and ash was still tucked in its place in one of her many pockets. She shrugged on her robe as she stumbled back toward the cell in which Zarina and her two daughters were imprisoned.

Boudreaux was a mess. The adrenaline that had powered him out of the gunk and into action was wearing off now, and he realized how much pain he was in. He could barely talk. At least a few ribs were broken. He was winded. He had a terrible headache. His torso armor and silver sword were gone. And he was completely saturated in filthy goo.

"That was amazing, guys," Gnome whistled through his teeth, as he and Waif emerged from the drainage tunnel. He peered over the edge into the gloppy pool as if to make sure the stone behemoth was really gone.

"We owe you our lives again, Boudreaux," Ohlen was saying, but his words trailed off as he looked distractedly past them toward the passage now bordered by just one stone statue.

Three ornately tattooed men spilled from the doorway. They were bald, bare from the waist up, and brandishing cruel-looking curved scimitars. They advanced slowly toward the bedraggled party, fanning out as they came.

Ohlen's senses prickled wildly. The arrival of these exotic warriors was one thing, and he could sense something far worse beyond.

Even so, a faint wet fleshy slapping sound behind him caused him to look over his shoulder. Staggering out of the gloom of the drainage tunnel behind them came dead and unblinking white eyes on a large naked and decaying body with stumps instead of hands.

*Two new arms had erupted from his flesh there, one on each side.
But they were not human arms, they were segmented crablike
exoskeleton arms ending in enormous pincers.*

Chapter Twenty-Seven
BLISTER, BURN, AND STING

———————

Arden could tell immediately they were good fighters. They moved low to the ground and advanced warily in a formation that both protected their blind sides and corralled their quarries. At no time did any joint move beyond its mid-range; they were all coil and potential, predators ready to strike.

Gnome was off. Dagger in his teeth, he flew easily up the curving walls and awaited the advance. Clinging like a spider to the ancient stone, he surveyed the scene unfolding beneath.

What the hell? The warrior in the center seemed to be glowing.

The tattoos—are they... moving?

The tattoos were, indeed, moving and glowing within the skin of the fighter in the middle. As gnome studied the three more closely, he realized that the skins of all the mysterious men were swimming with complex webs of snaking, slithering lines. But only the one in the middle was glowing, as if the thick dark lines had turned to molten magma flowing on the surface of his skin.

Boudreaux was closest to the glowing warrior in the middle. Stuffing back down the pain in his head and his chest, he unsheathed the large dwarven sword still strapped to his waist and stepped stiffly toward the advancing menace, sword tip low, body held intentionally too tall.

"I've had a bad day, guys, can we not do this right now?" he queried loudly to the room at large, in his best exasperated plea.

No response beyond cold, dark stares, and their continued wary approach.

But approach was exactly what Boudreaux was hoping for. The scimitar of the glowing guy, held loosely yet in response to Boudreaux's casual stance, came within reach.

Boudreaux seized his opening. Lunging fast and low with his right leg first, Boudreaux exploded outward with a backhand strike to the underside of the attacker's curved blade. He sunk the power from his legs and back and arms into swinging the heavy dwarf blade, and the other's scimitar flew into the air like a projectile out of his tattooed hand. It arced high into the air and landed with a clatter on the far side of the room.

A lot of other things happened in the short time it was in flight.

Boudreaux's surprised opponent yawned impossibly wide and began to crack open at the many tattooed seams on his skin. Through the orifices he emitted a blazing yellow-orange blast of sunlight-bright, furnace-hot radiation. Boudreaux was knocked to the ground instantly where he curled up into a ball, his bare torso hopelessly blistering, unintelligible moans escaping between the fists that protected his face.

Gnome watched the scene unfold from his perch. It was an excellent trick. As an accomplished illusionist himself, Gnome had to concede that the burning, glowing, fiery display was very impressive. His experience allowed him to see it for what it was, of course, but poor Boudreaux had not been so fortunate. His mind was so thoroughly convinced he had been terribly burned that it made the wounds manifest on his body.

Ohlen was just turning around when he was hit hard in the chest by the soggy, rotten shoulder of the undead fiend he had first met on the rock outside the Westwood forest. He landed on his back with the heavy, cold corpse on top of him, pinning him to the ground. It immediately began pummeling his face with its stump arms.

Even as he tried desperately to defend himself, Ohlen was conscious of how strange it felt to fight an emotionless opponent who experienced no pain and drew no breath. Ohlen hit back hard. He landed solid punches to the monster's ribs and face. He broke the brittle skin, and cracked bones. But the monster showed no reaction—it felt like punching a cold carcass. Ohlen's eyes and nose were bloody, his left ear had gotten caught by the monster's exposed radial bone and was torn, his teeth had begun cutting into his lips from all the brutality, but the monster did not stop. Unable to reach his weapon, Ohlen was quickly tiring.

The Islander combatant nearest Arden advanced menacingly along the edge of the sewage pool. Chaos reigned all around them. Boudreaux was disabled from a strange flash and something hideous had tackled Ohlen from behind. Arden drew the blade of his forefathers and swung its reassuring weight to warm his wrist as the attacker neared.

The Islander's blows came fast and furious. The curved blade and exotic, florid swordsmanship took some getting used to. Arden was able to read his attacker's motions, however, and parried several uncontested thrusts as he studied his opponent's tactics and looked for openings.

He found himself distracted by the crawling, mutating skin, however. The man was turning a dirt-brown color, and his bizarre tattoos were whirring in frenzy. Even as the cleaving blows continued in rapid succession, Arden's divided attention turned to horror as parts of the man's discolored head shifted and sunk rapidly into a deformation resembling a large misshapen potato. Fissures began opening like toothless mouths on his neck and arms. His eyes receded completely, leaving loose flapping lids that began oozing a thick black oily sludge.

It was disgusting.

Only when the relentless scimitar sliced off a bit of his left upper arm, did Arden regain full focus on the swordplay engaging him. Disturbed as he was at the nauseating transformation he had witnessed, it was time to go on the offensive.

His opponent was right-handed with weak outside defenses. Three rapid strikes from Arden's dominant left side put his opponent totally off balance. He gained ground but almost immediately wished he had not. The man had become a scimitar-wielding giant oozing pustule, and he had leaked black goo all over the floor. Arden's precious boots were now slipping in it and beginning to smoke.

Not again! Arden remembered the tentacular acid-worm that had melted part of his face, and his mind reacted viscerally. It was clear enough that whatever substance this thing was emitting, it was potently caustic.

The acid pus monster had retreated, leaving a wet trail glistening between them. Clearly this was its strategy. It would probably be just moments before the soles of Arden's boots were worn off completely and his feet began to liquefy.

Thinking quickly, Arden stopped his advance. He retreated instead to the edge of the sewage pool, and with his right hand surreptitiously on the hilt of his sheathed second sword, he made a show of dipping and rinsing his boots one at a time in the filth.

Just as he hoped, the seeping mess came shambling toward him to deal its death blow. But Arden's counter move was downright easy. He turned and parried with his left hand while swinging with his right to cleave the shriveled brown head-like mass from atop its gelatinous brown body.

His sword traveled easily through the distended flesh. The foul beast collapsed to the ground as if it had no bones left in it. Trembling, it leaked copious amounts of the steaming black bile onto the floor around it, which hissed as it flowed into the sewage below.

Weaponless, the glowing fiend leapt on top of Boudreaux and tried to pry Boudreaux's hands from his face to throttle his neck. Now Gnome could act. He launched himself from the domed ceiling toward the exposed undulating red-orange back.

It was one of the first things he had learned in the thieves' guild. Hide in the shadows. Wait for the opportunity to strike. When your mark is facing away from you, move silently to him and thrust your blade between the top two vertebrae beneath the neck. Quick, clean, effective, instantly debilitating, and ultimately deadly.

Held two-handed before him, the tip of Gnome's dagger landed just before the rest of him. The force of his flight drove the weapon deep, precisely in the place he was aiming for, completely severing the spinal cord. The massive body jerked violently and then went rigid. The bright glow quickly began to fade.

But Gnome was not finished. He had to help Boudreaux understand that the pain afflicting him was not reality.

"It's not real, Boudreaux! It's not real!" He tried to reach around the giant comatose man lying on top of Boudreaux's fetal form to slap him as he shouted.

"It's not—"

But that was all Gnome managed to say before a stinging swat struck him from behind and sent him sailing through the air to slam hard into the stone wall, where he slumped unconscious.

With the acid pus monster still quivering at his feet, Arden took in the scene around him. Ohlen was struggling for his life beneath what looked like a handless dead corpse that had festered underwater for weeks before being hauled to the surface and reanimated. Ohlen's face and hands were so completely covered in blood that he was unrecognizable.

Boudreaux was catatonic beneath the limp body of the formerly glowing warrior who appeared to have died on top of him, his color drained.

Beyond Boudreaux was a new menace. It had flicked Gnome like an insect into the wall where he now lay unconscious. This man's tattoos had turned into horizontal lines on his chest spaced wide in the middle but converging into thick mottled ropes at the bottom of his ribcage. Two new arms had erupted from his flesh there, one on each side. But they were not human arms, they were segmented crablike exoskeleton arms ending in enormous pincers.

If that weren't enough, towering behind him twitched a barbed scorpion tail. The thick trunk extended from the Islander's back and caused him to hunch forward awkwardly as it hogged skin and sinew to support the treacherous appendage.

Arden had a decision to make: help Ohlen with the undead fiend, or engage the scorpion man before his friends were massacred.

Before he could act, though, a new player arrived. Through the archway glided a tall blonde man in dark crimson robes. He had dark lines under his eyes, and while he may have been handsome at one time, his emaciated face now projected only hatred.

This cannot happen! Ohlen screamed in his mind, as bloody snot and drool extended in viscous ropes from his broken face to the floor.

Chapter Twenty-Eight
WATER, POISON, AND FIRE

Damn you, Waif. That's what his father used to say.

The day his mother left their home for good after too many beatings, too little food, and far too little love, his father drank and raged and yelled. *Damn you, Waif.*

The day his father cut off the forefinger and middle finger of his left hand at the mill, he stumbled home, having gotten drunk before even tending the wound properly, and gesticulated wildly, bloodily at his terrified son. *Damn you, Waif,* he howled.

Waif got caught the first time he stole something. He was desperately hungry and crept to the baker's stall at the market to nick a roll from a small pile still warm from the hearth. The baker chased him, shouting, all the way home. Waif ate the roll as he ran, too hungry even to wait, or to give it back. When he got home, his father listened stonily to the baker's ranting but offered no compensation. And when the baker, red-faced and fuming, finally stomped away, his father muttered weakly, *Damn you, Waif.*

Waif was feverish, sweating profusely, delirious. The filthy gory rat bite on his arm had turned into a raw sea of burning pus. A scene swam before his half-open eyes...even his wildest and most vivid nightmares had never approached anything remotely like this.

Waif had left home as a boy just shy of his eighth birthday. He lived on the streets and stole to survive before finding a home in The Den. The thieves trained him, fed him, sheltered him, and gave him structure. But never once did he receive what he needed most.

Until Gnome followed him that day.

You're a good rogue, Waif, Gnome had said. A compliment. A compliment paid by a stranger without calculation. It was a moment of generosity, of affection, even. This was so foreign that Waif had no reaction at all that day. But the warmth of that one small phrase grew into hope within him, a hope that someday he might actually belong.

And now Gnome lay wounded against a grimy wall. The blow had knocked him unconscious, though he now seemed to be stirring feebly.

A frightening, tall blonde man in dark red robes had floated— not walked—into the room. *Am I dreaming this?* His gaunt face was a mask of hatred as he surveyed the scene before him. The man pulled some shimmering garment over himself and disappeared entirely from view.

Yes, I must be dreaming, Waif thought.

His eyes drooped heavily closed.

It's not real, Boudreaux! Gnome's shouts penetrated the thick wall of burning pain that had become Boudreaux's reality. The hard stone beneath him felt cold. *Cold!* The blast he had experienced made him feel like he could never again feel cold as long as he lived. Yet the stone was cold beneath him.

It's not real, Boudreaux!

Boudreaux began to understand. He opened his eyes in time to see Arden bounding directly over him, swords drawn. He saw his friend rushing a hideous hybrid scorpion man, and Boudreaux willed his arms to move and push aside the heavy dead body that pressed down on him.

Cords of shredded muscle grew unnaturally out of the scorpion man to support the appendages that had erupted from his skin. His compact, hunched form was all weaponry, with two clawed arms, beneath a blade-wielding set of powerful human arms, and a stinging tail bobbing menacingly overhead.

Arden was having trouble even getting an attack in. He dodged the slices, snaps, stings, and punches like some manic dancer on a bed of hot coals.

Boudreaux was on his feet, running. By the time he arrived, Arden's midsection had been grasped by the monster's right pincer, and he was yelling and beating wildly on the claw, with the hilts of both swords.

Dodging a vicious lash from the tail, Boudreaux launched himself onto the smooth segmented crab arm that held his friend. Immediately he felt the other set of vise-like pincers closing around his own right leg.

"Take the man-parts, Arden, I'm on the crab," he grunted.

The sheer exoskeleton made it hard to get a good hold on the

Islander's appendages. Boudreaux turned his attention to the claw that was grasping at his leg. He grabbed both sides and twisted violently. There was a loud crack and the claw, along with part of the arm, came free in his hands.

Nearly suffocating from the pressure on his abdomen, Arden focused on the Islander's human arms and scimitar. It was extremely awkward—being squeezed and lifted slightly off the ground, while at the same time having Boudreaux's huge muscular form laboring beneath and between him and his foe. But fortunately this was awkward for the scorpion man as well, and they were too close for his lethal stinger to be of use.

Arden focused his double-bladed attack on the scimitar. The Islander was strong but he was no match for Arden's speed and skill. Even so, Arden took a nasty left hook to his jaw from the man's weaponless fist. Having pummeled the blade hand into weak submission, Arden leveled a blow at his opponent's left shoulder. He did not cut the arm off completely, but his sharp blade sunk deep into the taut tissue.

This happened at precisely the moment that Boudreaux cracked off the other segmented arm beneath him. Arden was still wearing the pincer and half of the arm connected to it, and the two men clattered to the floor on top of one another.

The mutant man struggled to stay upright. His left arm hung limply at his side, having been very nearly cut asunder. Both of his scorpion arms had been torn off, and he stumbled for stability, using his scimitar briefly to prop himself up.

Neither Boudreaux nor Arden would know for a long time why the clawed gashes appeared on their chests out of nowhere. It would be months later, in a casual conversation with X'andria, that they would put it all together. But just as they were recovering from the fall, and readying themselves to stand and finish off the abomination before them, they felt their flesh sliced deeply by the air itself, and blood began to flow.

The scorpion man staggered backward a few paces, creating just enough distance to utilize his freakish stinging tail.

Ohlen was finished. He had no strength left in him. He stopped fighting.

As soon as his body went limp, the undead creature on top of him stopped fighting, too. Instead it foraged for the leather satchel Ohlen carried over his shoulder, now pinned beneath him and steeped in sticky blood.

The beast flipped him over and looped a stumped arm inside the thick leather strap. With a violent yank, the strap broke and Ohlen's bag came free.

Just like before, at the rock where he had meditated, the creature single-mindedly searched for his ivory case.

It extracted the ivory case.

Ohlen, gasping for breath, began calling desperately upon the reserves behind his reserves.

It was fumbling with the case now—trying to open it.

Ohlen rolled painfully onto his side and tried to push himself onto all fours.

Somehow the handless monster had opened the case. The orbs were out. They were cradled in the dead flesh of its forearms, which it held together to form a trough.

This cannot happen! Ohlen screamed in his mind, as bloody snot and drool extended in viscous ropes from his broken face to the floor.

X'andria sprinted into the horrific scene. Boudreaux and Arden lay prone in a pile on the floor before a huge semi-human scorpion. Behind them, Ohlen was barely recognizable on his hands and knees near a monster she could not identify. Gnome was slumped by an unconscious boy near the wall.

She was rushing to aid Ohlen when her sharp eyes picked up something else in the space.

First she noticed the foul water stirring in the pool of sewage, which swirled unnaturally, like unseen hands were pulling and sculpting the fluid into a living corporeal entity. X'andria knew of only one way that elements could be manipulated: it required a controller.

Eyes darting, she detected the ripple in the air nearby. Although it was the faintest of wavy interruptions in light, she was not fooled.

Precious blood was pouring from her friends. Their savaged bodies were tortured and exhausted. She thought of the terror of Zarina and her girls, of the husband that Zarina had told her was most surely dead now.

And it made X'andria angry.

Holding her silk pouch tightly, she funneled her fury into fire. She fed it with her mind, fueled it with the torment she had experienced as a captive, fanned it with her desire for revenge.

Flame belched from X'andria's entire body. It leapt from her toes, from her knees, from her waist, from her chest and shoulders and fingers. Blue-white searing energy exploded out of her mouth and her eyes and her ears. With the intensity of rage she focused the incendiary blast into a jet of flame that sped through the space and engulfed the coward sheltering in invisibility near the pool.

Screams and flames erupted out of the nothingness. But quickly a burning man emerged. He was frantically pulling off flaming garments, screaming and coughing, his blond hair burning.

Elias? It can't be! X'andria's stomach lurched.

He was barely recognizable from just two days earlier. Nearly hairless, with charred and blistering skin, his piercing blue eyes stared back at her.

But he was different now. Where before he was all about intelligence and ambition, now he projected only hate and superiority.

His leering features twisted in recognition. The watery conjuration looming behind him splashed back down into formlessness.

I cannot let this happen! Ohlen forced himself to crawl.

The monster was sliding itself forward toward a burning man who had appeared out of nowhere. Ohlen grabbed for the sheathed sword still attached to him. Attempting to stabilize himself on one weak hand caused him to pitch forward onto his ruined face, his other arm buckling.

Lying powerless with his face pushed into the ground, he fumbled to unsheath his sword. Accomplishing that, he slid and scraped the weapon along the floor so that both hands were again in front of him, one of which now held a weapon.

Ohlen pushed himself back onto his hands and knees and willed himself to pursue the shambling monster before him. With a desperate lunge, he extended flat and drove the point of his sword through the calf muscle of the creature's left leg. Holding the hilt with both hands, Ohlen rolled onto his back to leverage as much tissue as possible from the decayed leg.

Ohlen could not see how effective his effort was, but he heard the stuttering flap of heavy feet and knew that damage was done. Lying on his back, he could only see toward the mouth of the drainage tunnel through which they had entered. He saw Waif, white, glistening and unconscious on the ground. He saw Gnome just teetering into a standing position.

"Gnome!" Ohlen yelled. It was the last of his strength. "Gnome. Please!"

And all went dark for Ohlen.

Boudreaux struggled to extricate himself from Arden. Arden began prying loose the giant claw still clinging to his midsection.

"Incoming!" Boudreaux yelled, and he rolled to the side.

The scorpion tail smacked into the ground right where he had been moments before, leaving a shiny patch of bright green venom steaming on the mark.

Arden was still freeing himself when the second attack came whipping mercilessly downward. And it would have hit him, too. But the instant before impact, the inert body of the formerly glowing mutant warrior sailed lightning-fast to hover directly above him. The tip of the savage stinger penetrated through the Islander's suspended body, glistening cruelly with blood and poison, before retracting back into the air.

The hovering corpse then went spinning through space and hit the scorpion man hard in the chest and face knocking him backward onto his huge tail.

X'andria—eyes still burning orange with patches of flame dotting the floor surrounding her—had adjusted her focus to the scorpion man, gold loop held aloft.

"I've got this," Boudreaux spat, and he pounced on the maimed and flailing scorpion assailant.

"Arden!" X'andria yelled, and she pointed to Elias, smoking on the far side of the room.

"Mordimer!"

The shriek was bloodcurdling. Sunk into that sound was the anguish of a mother who has lost the father of her children, the horror of a wife who has lost her husband to violence, the panic of a human being witnessing hell on earth.

And it stopped. The walking corpse that had been Mordimer turned to the sound, turned to the vision that had been its last comfort in life. The white eyes, without pupils, rested blankly on Zarina, on the two girls cowering behind her legs.

And then it continued to amble forward toward Elias, with its prizes finally collected.

But the pause lasted just long enough to give Gnome time to rush up from behind. He jumped and sailed, feet-first through the air, landing a powerful blow to the monster's broad back.

Chapter Twenty-Eight

It pitched forward.

And the marbles flew into the air.

Elias was still staring in outrage and disbelief at X'andria when the marbles hit him.

One landed on his left side, about where his stomach was. The other landed just above his right knee.

They sprung to life. Hundreds of barbed blades sprouted from both orbs and they cut and pulled and burrowed their way beneath his skin, blood spraying from both wounds.

He sunk to his knees as they swam through him. It was simultaneously the greatest pain and the greatest pleasure he had ever felt.

As Arden ran across the room, the whole terrible scene unfolded in slow motion. The orbs arcing through the air; Gnome toppling behind them; the undead beast grasping in space with its stumps as it fell forward; the orbs landing and spinning their way into the vile man's charred flesh.

Elias' screaming stopped and the shiny fathomless black eyes clicked open just as Arden arrived.

He did not hesitate.

Using both swords like a giant pair of scissors, Arden separated Elias' head from the perforated ruination of his body.

X'andria called upon the element of fire
for a third and final time that day.

Chapter Twenty-Nine
BLOOD

_____

Arden's arms were still fully extended, and Elias' head was just sliding away, when the orbs spun back into action in search of living flesh. As his kneeling body slumped forward onto the ground, they whirred throughout their host, liquefying as they swam, until there was nothing left of Elias but a large puddle expanding around a severed head, with two black orbs glistening idly in the midst.

With Elias' death so, too, ended the animation of Mordimer's corpse. The miserable lacerated and dismembered hulk fell heavily to the floor. Zarina, sobbing hysterically, rushed across the room to his side. Her daughters hovered nervously behind.

It was a catastrophic scene. Boudreaux stood up in the thrashed remains of the scorpion man. Arden, turning away from the gore before him, wiped and stowed his blades. Gnome, not bothering to stand, inched backward to Ohlen, who weakly moaned something unintelligible at the ceiling.

X'andria lifted Ohlen's ivory case with her will. It sailed across the room and plopped into the muck that had been Elias. One by one she carefully levitated each of the orbs into the case, and clicked it tightly shut to seal them in.

"Oh," moaned Ohlen more audibly, "that is so much better."

"We need to get you to the surface," Gnome said, "and Waif and the ladies, too."

Boudreaux stepped across the still scorpion tail, now broken at an odd angle, and approached X'andria.

"Did you do that, X'andria, with the fire and the flying dead guy?" he asked in amazement. "That was unbelievable."

X'andria nodded and flashed the faintest of smiles through the dried mud still crusting her face.

"We are not finished here," Ohlen mumbled.

"Oh, we're about as finished as we could possibly be," Gnome replied. "You should see what Arden did to the creep over there."

X'andria walked toward what remained of Elias.

"It was Elias, Boudreaux," she admitted coolly.

"What?" Boudreaux asked quizzically. "What was who?"

"This guy," she indicated the head and puddle, "was that guy I met at the Emporium that you thought was a creep." She laughed bitterly.

Ohlen propped himself up onto his left elbow. "We are not finished here," he said again, more loudly this time.

"What's up, Ohlen?" Arden asked, coming closer.

"There's something down there," Ohlen indicated the hallway with a twist of his head.

"Can you even walk?" Gnome asked sincerely.

"I'll manage," Ohlen grunted, moving shakily to a sitting position.

"What about the crying lady and these girls?" Boudreaux blurted out, as though they were not standing right next to him. "And Waif?" he added.

"I can hide them until we return," Gnome conceded, as he stood up, still eyeing Ohlen skeptically.

Boudreaux picked up Waif's inert body and deposited it near Zarina, still holding her vigil over her dead husband's body. "Now you girls need to stay close to your mom until we get back," Gnome said in a voice so gentle that none of them, especially Gnome, would have expected it to pass his lips.

Gnome paced around them in a wide circle. He took in the dreary surroundings on all sides. With the others looking on curiously, he reached into his tunic and produced a brown bundle of dried leaves.

"Hey, X'an," he called. She stood abruptly across the room where she had been stuffing something into her robe. "Could I get some help lighting this?"

"Sure," she called brightly and walked carefully around the perimeter of the Elias pool. With her silk bag in her left hand, she pinched the top of Gnome's leaf bundle, and it began to glow brightly with flame—which he immediately blew out.

Gnome grew silent and began waving the now-smoking incense in complex patterns in the air. Boudreaux and Arden watched in confounded silence as the figures on the ground in front of them began to disappear in a haze of hypnotic wavy patterns seemingly generated by the environment around them.

With Gnome's camouflaging illusion completed, they began walking toward the hallway.

"What should we do with this, Ohlen?" X'andria called. She was pointing at the ivory case.

"Would you take it, Arden?" Ohlen asked, indicating Arden's intact leather bag.

"That's where they were holding Zarina and me," X'andria pointed down a passageway to the left as if leading a tour. "But I don't think there was much else down there."

In about fifty feet they reached a short flight of descending stairs, then another, and then another. Ohlen leaned heavily on Boudreaux as they walked, and he bypassed several doors and corridors, intent on something further ahead.

"This is it," he finally whispered, before a closed wooden door.

X'andria loaded three darts into her left hand. Gnome slunk to the side, dagger clamped tightly in his teeth. With a wordless glance, Boudreaux and Arden agreed that Arden would lead and Boudreaux would support and protect Ohlen at the rear.

Arden blasted the door open with a sharp kick of his boot and rushed into the tiny room beyond, blades aloft.

The chamber glowed dimly. Two guttering candles, one on a desk in the corner, another on a short table in the middle, flickered weakly in the breeze generated by the door opening.

Warm and sickly. It took Boudreaux a moment to name it, but the closest memory he had to this odor was hog-slaughtering day when he was a boy. His master would give him a knife and a number. His job was to go into the pen and kill that many hogs. He chased the huge beasts around the pen, and killed them as quickly as he could, which was never very quick. On hot summer days, the heat and hog's blood, and sweat and muck all mixed together, smelled a bit like this abysmal place.

"What the hell is this?" It was Gnome. No one had even noticed him enter, yet he stepped out of a dark shadow into the very center of the room. He had a sickened look on his face.

Boudreaux led Ohlen inside and they all crowded around.

A shriveled pile of oily black skin, it looked like a soft prune the size of a large dog. It moved, pulsing slightly.

And it was looking at them with ruby eyes of pure fire, set above a pursed hole that might have been a toothless mouth.

"Ugh," X'andria groaned, holding her nose.

"Evil," Ohlen replied simply. "We need the book over there, and the scrolls, anything with writing on it. Then we must incinerate this blight upon the earth."

"With pleasure," came X'andria's nasal response, still holding her nose.

Arden and Boudreaux cleared the table of the book and two parchments, leaving behind various jars and one nasty-looking black serpentine blade.

With all of them safely out of the room, X'andria called upon the element of fire for a third and final time that day. She saw Elias, that smart handsome young man. She saw his ambition pulling him into darkness. She knew that it was this darkness, this foul evil before her, that had ultimately destroyed him and countless others in the process.

And the fire bled from her feet onto the floor and raced along the stone to the base of the blubbery mass. As soon as the flames reached it, the sac lurched to the side. An otherworldly noise burbled out of it almost like a prolonged flatulent roar.

Chapter Twenty-Nine

It did not burn, but the sac did begin to expand. With flame all around it, the heaving expanding mass became translucent and the liquid inside glowed red as it started to boil. The burbling reached a fever pitch, as the furious roaring mixed now with gurgled belching. Liquid and steam began spewing from the shapeless maw.

The sac grew still larger, more taut. X'andria's fury pumped mercilessly into the flames at its base, and the others crowded around to peer through the door, revolted and mesmerized at the same time.

And then it blew apart. The boiling blood of Mordimer, of the elderly shopkeeper, of all the Atolians, and of Elias himself, blasted apart the hellish sack that had robbed them of their dignity and of their lives.

Bits of membrane spattered everywhere along with the blood and the two rubies. X'andria was covered in gunk. They all were. It was revolting, but not so bad as to keep her from reaching surreptitiously into the slurry on the ground, and plucking a ruby that lay winking up at her. She slipped it into one of her many pockets.

Far away, Ruprecht stumbled his way through the dark forest. He did not know where he was going. It did not matter so long as he would never have to see Boudreaux again. Or any of them. He was so ashamed, so confused.

He thought of killing himself. But he lacked the courage to do it. And there was that horrid voice. That tiny persistent nag reminding him, *If you die, Ruprecht, you will never taste that glorious power again.*

So he ran. He would hide. Perhaps he could starve in some black hole somewhere. He more than deserved it for all the trouble he had caused.

And in this desperate state Ruprecht had a vision: a blinding light appeared suddenly before him and then receded to a mere outline shimmering in the night.

.

And coming soon

MERIDEN

BOOK THREE OF TINDER & FLINT

By
Matthew Hinsley

Art by
Billy Garretsen

A special preview...

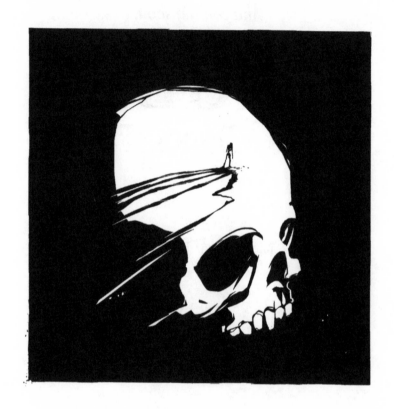

Many more months would pass before the bony black silhouette slipped past those very same bars—leaving behind only frost made by the complete and utter absence of good.

Chapter One
LEOPOLD

---

27 years ago...

It was not the first time his skin had been pierced with a blade.

Even through his drunken stupor and the haze of semi-consciousness he could sense the cowardly nature of the thrust. The tip pushed lamely against his skin at first, like a child testing chill in the water with his toe, before plunging in.

But plunge it did.

Once it entered his abdomen it moved more swiftly through his guts. It bit dully into his spine, before, with a shove, it altered course and found the path of least resistance out his back.

The painful acid warmth mixed and sloshed inside him, chasing the blade's path like hounds on a traitor's trail. The pungent smells of wine and bile engulfed him.

He was dying quickly. His life was dribbling out behind him in spurts. His strength was already leaving him. He had only enough left for one last look.

He wrenched open his left eye.

She was laughing. Candlelight flickered in her eyes as if the flames themselves were burning inside. Bertrand Ingroff, already bent to her will, heaved awkwardly against the hilt of the blade, like it was a shovel that's struck a root in the earth. Carlton lingered warily behind them, jug of wine in hand, with a nervous look as though he would be having a really good time so long as the man on the other end of his brother's blade died quickly and did not make too much of a mess.

A benefit of dying is the deadening of physical sensation. The agony was fading like a moon that has yet to leave the sky though the sun has risen. Leopold's body was convulsing involuntarily, further depleting itself of precious fluids.

But none of that mattered anymore. All that mattered was Estela. The pain wracking his body was nothing next to the flaying of his spirit by her treachery. Her laughter wrapped around the boy's cold steel like snakes of molten ore. Her deceit exploded like white-hot needles inside him, swimming through every inch of him, punishing him mercilessly with the burning wrath of her vengeance.

Leopold's eye shuddered and drooped closed.

He would never breath again. His heart stopped beating forever.

But the *Southern Sorcerer* did not cease to exist.

The bastards celebrated that night. They celebrated in front of him as only drunken boys and girls will do. And they laughed. She laughed. At him.

There was something he clung to that night. Anyone else would have given in to death completely, would have passed meekly into the shadow. But there was something too important for Leopold to let go. He wanted it fiercely with all his being, and so he desperately flung his magic out into the black void of his extinguishing mind to capture it. And by some miracle, aided by a mysterious flicker of red-hot power, his erratic lines of magic strained and hooked into something solid.

Even as his body cooled, his consciousness clutched his prize like a raft at sea. As Estela and Carlton and Bertrand reveled long into the night, feeding him with the sounds and smells of their ecstasy, he shivered atop it like a rat on debris from a wrecked ship. Ever so slowly it grew in him, and he in it, long after they carried him into the bowels of Ingroff Castle and cast his sunken old body onto the decaying pile of their many other victims.

The thing he held onto was hatred.

Leopold willed himself to subsist on earth for hatred alone.

Several years passed before Leopold had another coherent thought. His flesh quickly putrefied and sloughed away, feeding the many slithering things that bred in the growing tortured pile made of the Ingroff brothers' tragic conceit.

Hatred echoed faintly in the corpses of the fallen all around him. Hate for the wrongful persecution of their brothers and sisters and parents and children. There were other things too, valor and love and passion and conviction, but these things were of no interest to Leopold's new creeping existence.

His consciousness reawakened and clawed its way out of the black muck of his mind the day Carlton was killed. The death was too swift for the spoiled, deceitful boy who had watched as his brother murdered Leopold in his sleep. In flashes, though, Leopold glimpsed her labors over Carlton's body to reanimate it. He saw her toil, her gagging at the bloated corpse, her hopelessness and despair, and these things fueled flickers of maniacal glee within him.

Then she, her resurrected monster, and the sniveling Bertrand, all died at the hands of the mobs. He dimly registered their deaths, but the extinguishing of their pitiful souls was nothing compared to the glory of the marauding villagers' rage-fueled hysteria.

Every sense was filled at once with the deliciousness of their fury. So much so that Leopold was just barely aware of his own small son, Elias, scrabbling his way desperately through the dungeons, across the pile of death, over Leopold's own bones, to sneak away between the bars of the secret iron grate deep beneath the castle.

Many more months would pass before the bony black silhouette slipped past those very same bars—leaving behind only frost made by the complete and utter absence of good.

ABOUT THE AUTHOR

Matthew Hinsley loves a story you can crawl right into, one that grabs hold and won't let go until the ride is over. He likes heroes you can root for, who do things you might do. He doesn't like villains at all...

He and his wife Glenda live in Austin, Texas.

ABOUT THE ARTIST

Billy Garretsen is an established video game designer and artist with over 100 game credits for mobile, console and PC. He loves to make art, music, and creating exciting worlds and characters. He has a terrible soft spot for '80s cartoons and fantasy.

CPSIA information can be obtained
at www.ICGtesting.com
Printed in the USA
LVHW04s1611200418
574264LV00001B/241/P